D1649495

CONNEC

Eclipse
Simon Armitage

Friendly Fire
Peter Gill

Simon Armitage was born in West Yorkshire in 1963.
In 1992 he was a winner of one of the first Forward
Poetry Prizes, a year later he was the *Sunday Times*
Young Writer of the Year, and in 1994 he received a
major Lannan Award. He has published six collections
of poetry as well as the autobiographical prose book,
All Points North. He works as a freelance writer and
broadcaster, and teaches at universities in this country
and the United States. In 1998 he co-edited *The Penguin
Book of British and Irish Poetry since 1945*. In 1999
he edited *Short and Sweet: 101 very short poems* for
Faber and Faber.

Peter Gill was born in 1939 in Cardiff and started his
professional career as an actor. A director as well as a
writer, he has directed over eighty productions in the
UK, Europe and North America. At the Royal Court
Theatre in the sixties, he was responsible for introducing
D. H. Lawrence's plays to the theatre. The founding
director of Riverside Studios and the Royal National
Theatre Studio, Peter Gill lives in London.

ACC. No: 02226273

CONNECTIONS

Eclipse
SIMON ARMITAGE

Friendly Fire
PETER GILL

faber and faber

STANLEY
THORNES

822.91408

First published in this edition 2001
by Faber and Faber Limited
3 Queen Square London WC1N 3AU
Published in the United States by Faber and Faber, Inc.,
an affiliate of Farrar, Straus and Giroux, New York
Eclipse was first published in *New Connections* in 1997
Friendly Fire was first published in *New Connections 99* in 1999

Typeset by Country Setting, Kingsdown, Kent CT14 8ES
Printed in England by Mackays of Chatham plc, Chatham, Kent

All rights reserved
Eclipse © Simon Armitage, 1997
Friendly Fire © Peter Gill 1999

The right of Simon Armitage to be identified as author of *Eclipse*
has been asserted in accordance with Section 77
of the Copyright, Designs and Patents Act 1988

The right of Peter Gill to be identified as author of *Friendly Fire*
has been asserted in accordance with Section 77
of the Copyright, Designs and Patents Act 1988

All rights whatsoever in this work, amateur or professional,
are strictly reserved. Applications for permission for any use whatsoever
including performance rights must be made in advance, prior to any
such proposed use. For *Eclipse* apply to David Godwin Associates,
14a Goodwin's Court, Covent Garden, London WC2N 4LL.
For *Friendly Fire* apply to Casarotto Ramsay Ltd., National House,
60–66 Wardour Street, London W1V 4ND. No performance
may be given unless a licence has first been obtained.

This book is sold subject to the condition that it shall not, by way of
trade or otherwise, be lent, resold, hired out or otherwise circulated
without the publisher's prior consent in any form of binding or cover
other than that in which it is published and without a similar condition
including this condition being imposed on the subsequent purchaser

A CIP record for this book
is available from the British Library

ISBN 0–571–20698–0 (Faber edn)
ISBN 0–7487–4290–5 (Stanley Thornes edn)

2 4 6 8 10 9 7 5 3 1

Contents

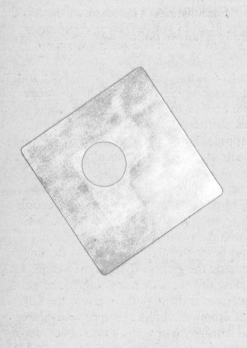

Foreword

The plays in this series were generated through a unique
and epic project initiated by the Royal National Theatre,
London, and funded by BT.

For many years the Education Department at the RNT
had been receiving calls from youth theatre companies
and schools asking us to recommend scripts for them
to perform. They were looking for contemporary,
sophisticated, unpatronising scripts with great plots and
storylines, where the characters would fit the age range
of the young people playing them. At that time, there
weren't many plays written for the 11 to 19 age group.
So we decided to approach the best writing talent around
and ask them to write short plays specifically for young
people.

In two-year cycles over a period of six years, we
created a portfolio of new plays and invited 150 schools
and youth theatres to choose the one that most excited
them. We then invited the participants to come on a
weekend retreat and work through the script with the
writer before producing the play in their home venue.
Some of those productions were then invited to one of
ten festivals at professional theatres throughout the UK.
Each two-year cycle culminated in a summer festival at
the Royal National Theatre, where the stages, back-stage
areas and foyers were ablaze with youthful energy and
creativity.

But the story doesn't end there. As we've discovered,
the UK isn't alone in demanding fantastic new scripts for
the youth market. A fourth cycle is already under way,
and this time the portfolio will include more contributions

from overseas. As long as there's a need, we will continue to commission challenging work to feed the intelligence, imagination and ingenuity of young people and the adults with whom they work.

Suzy Graham-Adriani
Royal National Theatre
July 2000

For more information on the writers and the work involved on the BT/National Connections project, visit: www.nt-online.org

ECLIPSE

Simon Armitage

Characters

Six friends:
Klondike, the oldest
Tulip, a tomboy
Polly and **Jane,** twins
Midnight, male, blind
Glue Boy, a glue-sniffer

Lucy Lime, a stranger

SCENE ONE

A police waiting-room. Seven chairs in a row, Glue Boy,
Polly and Jane, Midnight and Tulip sitting in five of them.
Klondike enters the room and sits down on one of the
empty chairs.

Klondike Tulip.
Tulip Klondike.
Klondike Midnight.
Midnight All right.
Klondike Missed the bus, then couldn't find it. Sorry I'm
late.
Midnight Are we in trouble?
Klondike Anyone been in yet?
Tulip No, just told us to sit here and wait.
Klondike Oh, like that, is it? Glue Boy.
Glue Boy Klondike.
Klondike Extra Strong Mint?
Glue Boy Bad for your teeth.
Midnight Klondike, tell me the truth.
Klondike And how are the split peas?
Polly and Jane We're the bees' knees.
Polly Yourself?
Klondike Could be worse, could be better.
Midnight Klondike, we're in bother, aren't we?
Klondike Three times. Who am I? St Peter?

Off, a voice calls 'Martin Blackwood'.

Midnight Me first? I thought we'd have time to get it
straight.
Polly Say as you speak . . .
Jane . . . speak as you find.

3

Klondike Say what you think, speak your mind. Clear?
Midnight Not sure.
Klondike Glue Boy, show him the door.
Tulip Klondike, why don't you tell him what's what? He's
   pissing his pants.
Klondike
   Let's all settle down. Midnight, stick to the facts.
   The oldies were up on the flat with the van,
   we were down in the crags.
   They were waiting to gawp at the total eclipse of the sun,
   we were kids, having fun.
   It was August eleventh, nineteen ninety-nine,
   they were pinning their hopes
   on the path of the moon,
   they were setting their scopes and their sights
   on a point in the afternoon sky
   where the sun put its monocle into its eye.
   The first and last that we saw of her. Right?
Tulip Right.
Polly and Jane Amen.
Midnight Just tell me again.

   Off, a voice calls 'Martin Blackwood'.

Tulip Stick to the facts. You were down on the sand . . .
Midnight
   I was down on the sand.
   The mothers and fathers were up on the land.
   Was it dark?

   Exit Midnight into interview room.

Tulip What a fart.
Klondike Oh, leave him. Blind as a bat. Sympathy vote.
   He'll be all right. Anyway, who's said what? Tulip?
Tulip No fear, kept mum like those two did.
Klondike Polly, Jane?
Polly Thought we'd keep schtum till you came.

4

Klondike Good move.

Glue Boy What about you?

Klondike What about me? What about you?

Glue Boy No, nothing.

Klondike Well, that's all right then.

Jane What can you hear through the crack?

Polly He was egging himself, I know that.

Tulip Shh. No, not a word.

Klondike Can you see through the glass?

Tulip Give us a leg-up . . . No, it's frosted.

Polly Moon came up. Sun was behind.

Jane Nothing to say. Nothing to hide.

Klondike Correct. Let's all get a grip. No need for anyone
losing their head.

Tulip The copper who came to the house said we're in this
up to our necks . . .

Klondike
FOR CRYING OUT LOUD . . .
They were up on the tops,
we were down in the rocks.
Stick to the facts.
Pax?

Tulip Pax.

Polly and **Jane** Pax.

Glue Boy Pax.

Klondike Stick to what we know and we'll all be fine.
Now, a moment's silence for Lucy Lime.

All For Lucy Lime.

SCENE TWO

A police interview room.

Midnight
Martin Blackwood, they call me Midnight –
it's a sick joke but I don't mind. Coffee

5

please, two sugars, white – don't ask me
to say that I saw, I'm profoundly blind,
but I'll tell you as much as I can, all right?

Cornwall, August, as you know. There's a beach
down there, seaside and all that, cliffs with caves
at the back, but up on the hill there's a view
looking south, perfect for watching a total eclipse
of the sun. The mums and dads were up on the top,
we were down in the drop – we'd just gone along
for the trip, killing a few hours. You see
it's like watching birds or trains, but with planets
and stars, and about as much fun as cricket
in my condition, or 3D. There was Glue Boy,
Polly and Jane, Tulip and Klondike and me.
Thing is, we were messing around in the caverns
when Lucy appeared. Her mother and father
were up with the rest of the spotters; she wasn't
from round here. Thing is, I was different then,
did a lot of praying, wore a cross, went to church,
thought I was walking towards the light of the Lord –
when it's as dark as it is in here, you follow
any road with any torch. Lucy put me on the straight
and narrow. There's no such thing as the soul,
there's bone and there's marrow. It's just biology.
You make your own light, follow your own nose.
She came and she went. And that's as much as I know.

We were just coming up from one of the smuggler's
coves . . .

SCENE THREE

*A beach in Cornwall, 11 August. At the back of the beach,
a broken electric fence dangles down from the headland
above. There are cave entrances in the cliff face.*

*Polly and Jane are sitting on a rock, combing each
other's hair, etc. They are heavily made up and wearing
a lot of jewellery.*

Polly Your turn.

Jane OK. The three materials that make up
Tutankhamun's mask.

Polly Easy. Solid gold, lapis lazuli and blue glass.

Jane Yes.

Polly Hairbrush. Thanks.

Jane Now you.

Polly Proof of man's existence at the time of extinct
mammals.

Jane Er . . . artwork carved on the tusks of mammals.

Polly Correct.

Jane Nailfile. Thanks.

Polly These are a doddle. Ask me something harder.

Jane Who swam through sharks with a seagull's egg in a
bandanna?

Polly A bandanna?

Jane All right, a headband.

Polly The birdmen of Easter Island. Easy-peasy.

Jane Lemon-squeezy.

Polly Cheddar-cheesy

Jane Japanesy

Polly Pass me the compact.

Jane Your go, clever clogs.

Polly On the same subject. The statues were studded with
which mineral?

Jane Er . . . malachite. No, marble.

Polly No, white coral.

Jane Sugar. When's the test.

Polly Monday next I think he said.

Jane Oh, I should be all right by then. (*Pause.*) What time
do you make it?

Polly Twenty past. Another couple of hours yet, at least.

Jane Mine must be fast.

Polly Let's synchronize, just in case.

Jane It might be yours. Yours might be slow.

Polly I don't think so. Anyway, it's solar-powered – it's been charging up all summer.

Jane Look out, here come the others.

> *Klondike, Tulip and Glue Boy come running out of one of the caves. Glue Boy is sniffing glue from a plastic bag, and continues to do so throughout. Klondike wears a leather bag on his back and is carrying the skeletal head of a bull. Tulip is wearing Dr Marten boots and a red headscarf worn like a pirate.*

Klondike Bloody hell, it's a cow's skull.

Tulip How do you know it's not from a sheep?

Klondike You're joking. Look at the size of it. Look at the teeth. Some caveman's had this for his tea. Hey, girls, fancy a spare rib?

Polly Take it away, it stinks.

Jane And I bet it's crawling with fleas.

Klondike It's a skull, you pair of dumb belles, not a fleece.

Tulip He found it right at the back of the cave.

Klondike I reckon it fell through the gap in the fence – it's been lying there, waiting for me.

Polly It gives me the creeps.

Glue Boy It's a dinosaur. Ginormous Rex.

Klondike I'm going to frame it or something. Put it in a case.

> *Tulip takes off her red headscarf, unfurls it and uses it as a matador's cape.*

Tulip Come on, Klondike. Olé. Olé.

Polly Where's Midnight.

Tulip Still coming out of the hole. Let's hide.

Jane Don't be rotten. That'd be really tight.

Polly Why don't we just stay here like statues. He can't see us.

Klondike He'd hear us, though. He's got ears like satellite dishes.

Glue Boy Like radar stations.

Tulip Everyone scarper and hide.

Glue Boy Everyone turns into pumpkins when Midnight chimes.

Exit Glue Boy, Polly and Jane.

Tulip Wait, my scarf.

Klondike Leave it.

Exit Klondike and Tulip, leaving the scarf behind. Enter Midnight from the cave, wearing dark glasses, and a crucifix around his neck, which he holds out in front of him in his hand.

Midnight Klondike? Tulip? That skull, what is it?

Enter Lucy Lime.

Klondike? Glue Boy. Come on, don't be pathetic. Tulip? Tulip?

Lucy Selling flowers, are we?

Midnight Polly? Jane?

Lucy Penny Lane? Singing now, is it?

Midnight I'm Midnight. Who are you?

Lucy I'm twenty-to-three. Look. (*She makes the position of a clock's hands with her arms.*)

Midnight I can't look. I can't see.

Lucy Oh, you should have said. I'm Lucy. Lucy Lime.

Midnight I thought you were one of the others. They said they'd wait for me somewhere around here.

Lucy No, I'm not one of the others. And you can put that thing down. I'm not Dracula's daughter either.

Midnight What, this? Sorry. I'm a believer. It's Jesus, watching over.

Lucy Well, don't point it at me. It's loaded.

An animal noise comes out of one of the caves.

What was that? A bat?

Midnight More like Klondike messing about.

Lucy Klondike?

Midnight Him and Tulip and Glue Boy and the twins. We all came here in a van to do this star-gazing thing, or at least everybody's parents did, but it's boring.

Lucy So you've been exploring?

Midnight Yes. Pot-holing.

Lucy How did you . . .

Midnight Go blind?

Lucy Lose your sight, I was going to say.

Midnight Looked at the sun through binoculars when I was ten.

Lucy By mistake?

Midnight For a bet. Burnt out. Never see again.

Lucy Sorry.

Midnight Not to worry. I've got Jesus, and the truth.

Lucy Truth? What's that.

Midnight When you can't see, it's better to follow one straight path.

Lucy Oh, right. (*Pause.*) Do you want them to come back?

Midnight I told you, they're written off.

Lucy No, the others, I mean.

Midnight Oh, they won't. They think it's a good crack, leaving me playing blind man's buff.

Lucy Ever caught moths?

Midnight What have moths got to do with it?

Lucy Oh, nothing. (*She sets fire to the silk scarf and tosses it up in the air. It flares brightly and vanishes.*)

Enter Klondike, Tulip, Polly and Jane.

Klondike Midnight, what's going on?

Tulip We thought we saw something burning . . .

Polly Or a meteorite falling . . .

Jane A maroon or whatever they're called, like a rocket . . .

Klondike Or sheet lightning.

Glue Boy Air-raid warning. Keep away from the trees. The strike of midnight.

Midnight Er . . .

Lucy It was a will-o'-the-wisp.

Tulip Who the hell's this?

Midnight Er . . .

Lucy Lucy Lime. Mother and father are up on the top with your lot. I've been keeping your friend company – thought you'd be looking for him.

Klondike Er . . . that's right. We got separated.

Lucy Lucky I was around then. Wouldn't have wanted the electric fence to have found him.

Polly (*aside*) Strange-looking creature.

Jane Not pretty. No features. Hairy armpits, I bet.

Polly Yeah, and two hairy legs.

Midnight sits on a stone away from everyone else and puts on his Walkman.

Lucy Mind if I join you?

Klondike Sorry?

Lucy Mind if I stay?

Tulip Feel free. Free country.

Jane I'm bored. Let's play a game.

Klondike Let's trap a rabbit and skin it.

Polly You're kidding. Let's play mirror, mirror on the wall . . .

Jane Spin the bottle. Postman's knock.

Glue Boy Pin the donkey on the tail.

Lucy What about hide and seek?

Tulip British bulldogs. No, numblety peg.

Lucy What's that?

Tulip That's where I throw this knife into the ground between your legs.

Klondike I know. We'll play bets. I bet I can skim this stone head-on into the waves.

Polly We know you can. I bet if we had a vote, I'd have the prettiest face.

Jane I bet you'd come joint first.

Tulip I bet I dare touch the electric fence.

Klondike Easy, you've got rubber soles. What do you bet, Evo-Stik?

Glue Boy Tomorrow never comes.

Klondike Sure, you keep taking the pills.

Lucy I can get Midnight to tell a lie. That's what I bet.

Tulip Your off your head. He's as straight as a die.

Glue Boy Straight as a plumb-line.

Klondike You've got no chance. He's a born-again Mr Tambourine man. A proper Christian.

Polly Says his prayers before he goes to bed . . .

Jane Goes to church when it's not even Christmas.

Lucy I don't care if he's Mary and Joseph and Jesus rolled into one. He'll lie, like anyone.

Tulip What do you bet?

Lucy I bet this. Two coins together – it's a lucky charm – a gold sovereign melted to a silver dime.

Klondike It's Lucy Locket now, is it, not Lucy Lime?

Lucy It's worth a bomb.

Tulip We can sell it and split it. OK, you're on. I bet this knife that you're wrong.

Lucy I've no need of a knife. I'll bet you your boots instead.

Polly I'll bet you this bracelet. It's nine-carat gold.

Jane I'll bet you this make-up case. It's mother-of-pearl.

Glue Boy I'll bet Antarctica.

Lucy You can do better than that, can't you?

Glue Boy OK, the world.

Tulip What do you bet, Klondike?

Klondike My skull.

Lucy Not enough.

Klondike And these Boji stones, from Kansas, under an ancient lake.

Lucy Not enough.

Klondike All right, if you win – which you won't – you can kiss this handsome face.

Lucy Everybody shake on it.

Klondike All for one, and once and for all.

Glue Boy And one for the road. And toad in the hole.

Lucy Glue Boy, is that your name?

Glue Boy One and the same.

Lucy Come with me, you're the witness.

Polly Why him? He doesn't know Tuesday from a piece of string.

Lucy Sounds perfect. Everyone else, keep quiet.

Lucy and Glue Boy approach Midnight. Lucy taps him on the shoulder.

Listen.

Midnight What?

Lucy Can you hear a boat?

Midnight Nope.

Lucy Listen, I can hear its engine. I'm certain.

Midnight I think you're mistaken.

Lucy There, just as I thought – coming round the point.

Midnight There can't be. Which direction?

Tulip (*to the others*) What's she saying, there's no boat.

Lucy Straight out in front. Plain as the nose on your face. See it, Glue Boy?

Glue Boy Er . . . ? Oh, sure.

Lucy It's a trawler. Is it greeny-blue, would you say?

Glue Boy Well, sort of sea green, sort of sky blue, sort of blue moon sort of colour.

Lucy I'm amazed you can't hear it, it's making a real racket.

Midnight Well, I . . .

Lucy Too much time with the ear-plugs, listening to static.

Midnight My hearing's perfect.

Lucy Fine. OK. Forget it.

Midnight I'm sorry. I didn't mean to be rude.

Lucy You weren't. I shouldn't have mentioned it. It's my fault – I should have thought. You can't hear the boat for the sound of the seagulls.

Midnight Seagulls?

Polly (*to the others*) There isn't a bird for miles.

Jane This is a waste of time. It's her who's telling the lies.

Lucy All that high-pitched skriking and screaming. Must play havoc with sensitive hearing like yours.

Midnight How close?

Lucy The birds? Three hundred yards, five hundred at most. Black-headed gulls, Glue Boy, don't you think?

Glue Boy Well, kind of rare breed, kind of less common, kind of lesser-spotted type things.

Lucy Don't say you're going deaf.

Midnight Who, me?

Lucy Glue Boy can hear them, and he's out of his head. Come on, Midnight, stop clowning around. I bet you can hear it all. I bet you can hear a cat licking its lips in the next town, can't you?

Midnight I don't know . . . I think sometimes I filter it out.

Lucy Yes, when you're half asleep. But listen, what can you hear now?

Midnight Er . . . something . . .

Lucy That aeroplane for a start, I bet.

Midnight Yes. The aeroplane.

Lucy I can't see it myself. Where would you say it was?

Midnight Er . . . off to the left, that's my guess.

Lucy What else? That dog on the cliff, half a mile back. Can you hear that?

Midnight Yes. The dog. Sniffing the air, is it? Scratching the ground?

Lucy Amazing. Wrap-around sound. What else? The boy with the kite?

Midnight
Yes, the kite.

The wind playing the twine like a harp.
It's a wonderful sound.

Lucy And Klondike and Tulip, coming back up the beach.
What are they talking about?

Midnight They're saying . . . this and that, about that
eclipse, and how dark and how strange it'll be.

Lucy And down by the rock pools, the twins?

Midnight Chatting away. Girls' things. Boyfriends, that
kind of stuff. It's not really fair to listen in on it.

Lucy You're not kidding. You're absolutely ultrasonic.
Glue Boy, how about that for a pair of ears?

Glue Boy Yeah, he's Jodrell Bank, he is.

Lucy And one last noise. A siren or something?

Midnight Car alarm.

Lucy No. Music.

Midnight Brass band. 'Floral Dance'.

Lucy No. It's there on the tip of my tongue but I just can't
place it. You know, sells lollies and things.

Midnight Ice-cream van. Ice-cream van. I can hear it.

Lucy You can?

Midnight Can't you?

Lucy No. Not any more. What was the tune?

Midnight Er . . . 'Greensleeves'.

Lucy 'Greensleeves', eh? Thanks, Midnight, that should
do it.

Midnight Sorry?

Tulip Nice one, stupid.

Midnight What? I thought you were . . .

Tulip Yeah, well, you know what thought did.

Polly Pathetic, Midnight.

Jane You should see a doctor, you're hearing voices.

Midnight But, all those noises . . .

Klondike She made them up, you soft bastard. I tell you
what, you should take more care of those ears.

Midnight Why's that?

Klondike 'Cos if they fall off, you won't be able to wear glasses.

Midnight I didn't invent them.

Polly You lying rat.

Jane You just lost us the bet, Dumbo. Do us a favour – stick to your Walkman.

Lucy Midnight, I'm sorry.

Midnight Get lost. Keep off me.

Polly Where are you going?

Midnight Anywhere away from here.

Klondike Well, get me a ninety-nine will you, when you're there.

Tulip And a screwball as well.

Midnight Go to hell.

Midnight takes off his crucifix and throws it in the direction of Lucy. Lucy picks it up and puts it in her bag.

Lucy Well, I think that clinches it, don't you? The bracelet, the case, the boots and the skull and the stone, if you please.

Everyone hands her the items. Lucy puts on the shoes and puts everything else in her bag.

Klondike Forgetting something?

Lucy I don't think so.

Klondike A kiss from me, because you did it.

Lucy No thanks, Romeo. I was only kidding.

Polly What a cheek. Not to worry, in the glove compartment I've got more jewellery, too good for that gold-digger.

Jane But you've got to hand it to her. I'll come to the car park to check out the courtesy light and the vanity mirror.

Exit Polly and Jane.

Glue Boy What did I bet?

Lucy The Earth.

Glue Boy I've left it at home in my other jacket. Double or quits?

Lucy No, I'll take it on credit.

Glue Boy A whole planet. In a top pocket.

Tulip Hey, where do you think you're going?

Lucy To see Midnight, make sure he's OK.

Tulip You've got a nerve.

Lucy Why? It was only a game.

Glue Boy Klondike, the sun . . .

Klondike Don't you think you've lost enough for one day?

Glue Boy No, the shadow. Here it comes.

Lucy It can't be. It's too early to start.

Tulip He's right, it's going dark. Klondike?

Klondike ECLIPSE, ECLIPSE. EVERYONE INTO POSITION. EVERYONE INTO POSITION.

Tulip We're short.

Klondike Who's missing?

Tulip Midnight. Gone walkabout. And the twins, where are the twins?

Klondike Get them back. Polly. Jane. POLLY. JANE.

SCENE FOUR

The police interview room. Polly and Jane make their statement, sometimes talking in unison, sometimes separately, one sister occasionally finishing the other sister's sentence.

Polly and Jane
　　They were up on the tops, we were down on the deck,
　　kicking around in pebbles and shells and bladderwrack.
　　They were watching the sky, we were keeping an eye

on the tide, hanging around, writing names in the sand,
turning over stones, pulling legs from hermit crabs.

We're two of a kind, two yolks from the same egg,
same thoughts in identical heads, everything half
and half, but it's easy enough to tell us apart:
I'm the spitting image; she's the copy cat.

They were up on the top looking south, we were down
on the strand looking out for something to do. She came
and she went in the same afternoon, saw the eclipse,
like   us,
but mustn't have been impressed, so she left. Straight up.
And a truth half told is a lie. We should know, we're a
Gemini.

Oh, yes, and we liked her style and the way she dressed.
We were something else before the daylight vanished.
Whatever we touched was touched with varnish.
Whatever we smelt was laced with powder or scent.
Whatever we heard had an earring lending its weight.
Whatever we saw was shadowed and shaded out of
sight.
Whatever we tasted tasted of mint.
Whatever we spoke had lipstick kissing its lips.
We were something else back then, all right, muddled
up,
not thinking straight, as it were. But now we're clear.

Same here.

SCENE FIVE

*The beach. Klondike, Tulip, Glue Boy and Lucy are
standing looking at the sky.*

Tulip False alarm. Just a cloud.

Klondike Thought so. Too early.
Tulip What now?
Glue Boy I-spy.
Tulip Boring. Hide and seek. Come on, Klondike, hide
and seek.
Klondike OK. Spuds up.
Lucy What, like this?
Klondike Yes, that's it.

*They all hold out their fists, with thumbs pointing
skyward.*

One potati, two potati, three potati, four,
five potati, six potati, seven potati, more . . .
Tulip
There's a party on the hill, will you come,
bring your own cup of tea and a bun . . .
Glue Boy
Ip dip dip, my blue ship,
sails on the water, like a cup and saucer . . .
Klondike
It's here, it's there, it's everywhere,
it's salmon and it's trout,
it shaves its tongue and eats its hair,
you're in, you're in, you're in . . . you're out.

The dipping-out lands on Lucy.

Tulip You're it.
Lucy OK, how many start?
Klondike Fifty elephants, and no cheating.
Glue Boy Fifteen cheetahs, and no peeping.
Lucy Off you go then.

*Lucy turns her back and begins counting. Exit Tulip
and Klondike.*

One elephant, two elephant, three elephant . . .
Glue Boy Filthy underpants and no weeping.

Klondike returns and drags Glue Boy off. Enter Polly and Jane.

Polly Hey, there's what's-her-face.

Jane What's she playing at?

Polly Practising her times-table by the sounds of it. Let's tell her to get lost.

Jane No, I've got a better idea. Let's give her a shock.

Lucy . . . fifty elephants. Coming ready or not.

Polly and Jane BOO!

Lucy Don't do that. You'll give someone a heart attack.

Polly We're the two-headed . . .

Jane . . . four-armed . . .

Polly . . . four-legged . . .

Jane . . . twenty-fingered monster from the black lagoon.

Lucy And one brain between the pair of you.

Polly Now, now. No need to be nasty.

Jane Yeah, no one's called you pale and pasty, have they?

Lucy I just meant that it's hard to tell you apart.

Polly We like it that way.

Jane It's scary.

Lucy Anyway, this is the natural look.

Polly What, plain and hairy?

Lucy No, pure and simple. Basically beautiful.

Jane Says who?

Lucy Says people. Boys. Men.

Jane You got a boyfriend then?

Lucy Yes. Someone. What about you two?

Jane No one to speak of . . .

Polly We're not bothered. All those round our way are filthy or ugly and stupid.

Lucy Maybe you should do what I did then.

Polly What was that?

Lucy Well,
three men fishing on the towpath wouldn't let me past;

called me a tramp, threw me in and I nearly drowned.
I was down in the weeds with dead dogs and bicycle frames.
Couldn't move for bracelets and beads and rings and chains.
Don't know why, but I ditched the lot in a minute flat,
took off my clothes as well: cuffs and frills and scarves,
heels and buttons and lace and buckles and shoulder-
    pads,
climbed out strip jack naked on the other bank, white-
    faced
and my hair down flat. The three men whistled and clapped
but I stood there, dressed in nothing but rain. They stopped
and threw me a shirt and a big coat, which I
wouldn't   take.
One of them covered his eyes, said it was somebody's fault;
a fight broke out and I watched. All three of them cried,
said they were sorry, said they were shamed. I asked them
to leave, and they shuffled away to their cars, I suppose,
and their wives. I put on the coat and shirt, walked home,
but never went back to dredge for the gold or the clothes.
This is me now. Be yourself, I reckon, not somebody else.

Jane What a story.

Polly Jackanory.

Lucy Well, that's what happened. You should try it. You might be surprised.

Jane You're kidding. Us?

Polly Not on your life.

Lucy Why not?

Jane How do we know we'd look any good?

Polly We wouldn't.

Lucy You would. Well, you might.
   Anyhow, better to look the way you were meant to be
   than done up like a tailor's dummy and a Christmas
   tree.

Polly
   Better to look like us
   than something the cat wouldn't touch.

Lucy No cat curls its nose up at good meat.

Polly
   No, but I know what they'd go for first
   if it's a choice between semi-skimmed or full-cream.

Lucy Suit yourselves.

Polly We will.

Lucy But don't blame me when you're twenty-three or
   thirty-four or forty-five, and left on the shelf.

Polly We won't.

Klondike (*off*) You haven't found us yet.

Lucy Am I warm or cold?

Klondike (*off*) Cold as a penguin's chuff.

Tulip (*off*) Cold as an Eskimo's toe.

Glue Boy (*off*) Yeah, cold as a polar bear's fridge. In a
   power cut.

Klondike and Tulip (*off*) Shut up.

Jane (*to Polly*) Why don't we give it a go?

Polly No.

Jane Why not?

Polly Because.

Jane It won't harm. Just for a laugh.

Polly I haven't put all this on just to take it all off.

Jane Come on, Sis, do it for me.

Polly What if we're . . . different?

Jane What do you mean?

Polly What if we don't look the same? Underneath?
Jane Don't know. Hadn't thought. Put it all on again?
Polly Straight away?
Jane Before you can say Jack Robinson. Before you can
say . . .
Polly OK.
Jane Lucy. We're going to give it a whirl.
Polly Just for a laugh, though. That's all.
Lucy Excellent. Down to the sea, girls. Down to the shore.
(*sings*)

Oh ladies of Greece
with the thickest of trees,
covered with blossom and bumble,
snip off the bees
and there underneath
two apples to bake in a crumble.

Oh ladies of France
with warts on your hands,
come down, come down to the waters.
And where you were gnarled
at the end of your arms
two perfect symmetrical daughters.

Oh ladies of Spain
at night on the lane
in nightshirts and mittens and bedsocks,
strip off those duds
and ride through the woods
on horses carved into the bedrock.

While singing, Lucy strips them of their jewellery and
some of their clothes, and washes their hair in the sea.
She puts the jewellery and a few choice items of clothing
into bag.

How does it feel?
Jane Unreal. I feel like someone else.

Lucy Polly?

Polly Not sure. Up in the air.

Jane I feel lighter and thinner.

Lucy Polly?

Polly See-through. Like a tree in winter.

Lucy You look great. You look like different people.

Polly Sorry?

Lucy I mean . . . you still look the same, alike. Just different types.

Jane Here come the others. See if they notice.

Polly Oh no. Let's hide.

Jane Too late. What shall we say?

Lucy Say nothing. Just smile. They'll only be jealous.

Enter Klondike, Tulip and Glue Boy.

Klondike Couldn't you find us?

Lucy No. You win.

Tulip We were down in the caves with the dead pirates.

Klondike How hard did you look?

Lucy Oh, about this hard. Feels like I've been looking for hours.

Tulip We were camouflaged.

Glue Boy Yeah, we were cauliflowers.

Tulip Oh my God.

Klondike What's up?

Tulip It's those two. Look.

Klondike Wow. I don't believe it.

Jane What's the matter with you? Never seen a woman before?

Tulip Never seen this one or that one. What happened? Get flushed down the toilet?

Lucy They've changed their minds.

Tulip You mean you changed it for them. That's all we need, three Lucy Limes.

Glue Boy Three lucky strikes. Three blind mice.

Polly Shut it, Glue Boy.

24

Klondike I think they look . . . nice.

Tulip Nice? They look like bones after the dog's had them.

Lucy They had a change of heart.

Glue Boy Heart transplant.

Klondike I think they look . . . smart. Sort of.

Tulip Yeah, and sort of not. They don't even look like twins any more. Don't look like anyone.

Polly I told you we shouldn't have.

Jane Don't blame me. You don't look that bad.

Polly Me? You should see yourself. You look like something out of a plastic bag.

Jane So what? You look like an old hag. You look like a boiled pig.

Tulip Glue Boy, what do they look like? Mirror, mirror on the wall . . .

Glue Boy
Mirror, mirror on the wall,
who's the worstest of them all . . .

Jane Glue Boy . . .

Glue Boy This one looks like a wet haddock . . .

Jane I'll kill you.

Glue Boy But this one looks like a skinned rabbit.

Polly Right, you've had it.

Polly and Jane pull Glue Boy's glue bag over his head and start to kick him. He wanders off and they follow, still kicking him.

Klondike They'll slaughter him.

Tulip He wouldn't notice.

Lucy What a mess.

Tulip Yes, and you started it.

Lucy Me? It was all fine till you came back and started stirring it. Now it's a hornet's nest.

Klondike Leave it alone. It'll all come out in the wash.

Lucy (*holding up some of the clothes left on the floor*)

What about these? Needles from Christmas trees.

Klondike Tulip, go and put leaves back on the evergreens.

Tulip Why me? What about her – Tinkerbell?

Klondike I don't think that'd go down too well. Please?

Tulip OK, give them here.

Lucy Take this, a brush for back-combing their hair.

Tulip Beach-combing more like. How kind.

Lucy That's me, sweetness and light. Lime by name, but sugar by nature. Isn't that right?

Klondike Eh? How should I know? Got everything?

Tulip S'ppose so.

Klondike Won't take a minute.

Tulip (*to Klondike, privately*) You'll wait here, won't you?

Klondike 'Course.

Tulip Don't let her . . .

Klondike What?

Tulip Doesn't matter.

Klondike Go on, what?

Tulip Talk to you, you know.

Klondike No. I won't do.

Tulip Don't let her . . . Lucy Lime you.

Klondike Don't be daft. Go on, I'll time you.

Exit Tulip.

Enjoying yourself?

Lucy I've had better.

Klondike Where are you from?

Lucy All over. (*Pause.*)
I'm a walking universe, I am.
Wherever the best view comes from,
wherever Mars and the moon are in conjunction,
wherever the stars and the sun are looking good from,
wherever the angles and the right ascensions and declinations
and transits and vectors and focal lengths and partial perigons

26

are done from, that's where I come from.
Traipsing round with mother and father. What about
you lot?

Klondike Yorkshire. Came in a van.

Lucy Bet that was fun.

Klondike I meant it, you know.

Lucy Meant what?

Klondike About that kiss. If you want to.

Lucy What about her? Don't you think she'd mind?

Klondike Tulip? No, she's all right. She's just . . .

Lucy One of the lads?

Klondike Something like that. Well, what about it?

Lucy Ever played rising sun?

Klondike Don't think so. How do you play it?

Lucy Well,
A light shines bright through a sheet or blanket,
somebody follows the sun as it rises,
it dawns at daybreak above the horizon,
the one looking east gets something surprising . . .

Klondike Really?

Lucy Something exciting. Something to break the ice with.

Klondike Let's try it.

Lucy Sorry, no can do. We need a torch for the sun.

Klondike (*producing a torch*) Like this one?

Lucy And we need a sheet.

Klondike (*taking off his shirt*) You can use this shirt.

Lucy And it needs to be dark. Sorry, can't be done.

Klondike I'll put this blindfold on. (*Without taking it off,
he lifts the bottom front of his T-shirt over his head.*)

Lucy OK, here it comes.

*Klondike kneels on the floor and holds his T-shirt up in
front of his face. Lucy, on the other side, presses the
torch against the shirt and raises it very slowly.
Klondike follows the light with his nose.*

Rain in the north from the tears of Jesus,

Rind in the west with its knickers in a twist;
Flies in the south sucking blood like leeches,
Sun coming up in the east like a kiss,
(*whispers*) from Judas.

Repeat.

SCENE SIX

The police interview room.

Tulip
When she left us for good I was nine or ten.
Ran off with the milkman, so Dad said. Ran off
with the man in the moon, as far as I care.
Grew up with uncles, cousins, played rugby-football,
swapped a pram for a ten-speed drop-handlebar,
played with matches instead, flags and cars, threw
the dolls on a skip and the skates on a dustcart,
flogged the frills and pink stuff at a car-boot sale,
burnt the Girl Guide outfit in the back garden,
got kitted out at Famous Army Stores and Top Man.
And Oxfam. I'll tell you something that sums it up:
found a doll's-house going mouldy in the attic –
boarded it up, kept a brown rat in it.
Put it all behind now, growing out of it, Dad says, says
I'm blossoming, and I suppose he must be right. Klondike?
No, not a boyfriend, more like a kid brother, really,
known him since as far back as I can remember.
Kissed him? Who wants to know? I mean no, Sir,
except on his head, just once, on his birthday.
Him and Lucy? Well, she took a shine to him,
he told her some things and I think she liked him.
She just showed up and wanted to tag along,
make some friends, I suppose, mess about, have fun;

she had a few tricks up her sleeve, wanted . . . all right,
if you put it like that . . . to be one of the group.
It's not much cop being on your own. Which was fine
by us. It's not that we gave it a second thought
to tell you the truth. She just turned up that afternoon
like a lost dog. She was one of the gang. Then she was
  gone.

SCENE SEVEN

The beach. Lucy and Klondike playing rising sun.

Lucy
  Rain in the north from the tears of Jesus,
  Wind in the west with its knickers in a twist;
  Flies in the south sucking blood like leeches,
  Sun coming up in the east like . . . piss.

Lucy throws water in his face.

Klondike You bitch.
Lucy Someting to break the ice, you see. It was a riddle.

Enter Tulip, unnoticed.

Klondike It was a swindle.
Lucy Oh, come on. You can take it. Here, dry off on this.
  (*She hands him his shirt and kisses him on the
  forehead.*)
Klondike You shouldn't joke.
Lucy What about?
Klondike Rhymes and religion. Old things. Things in the
  past.
Lucy I don't believe in all that claptrap.
Klondike It's just the way you've been brought up.
Lucy Yes, in the twentieth century, not in the dark.
  Anyway, what about your lot? They're up there

believing in science and maths.

Klondike No, with them it's the zodiac.

Lucy Oh, I see. It's like that.

Klondike They've come to take part, not take photographs.

Pause.

Lucy What's in the bag?

Klondike Bits and pieces.

Lucy Show me. Or is it a secret?

Klondike Just things I've collected.

Lucy Suit yourself. Only, I was interested.

Klondike Well, it's just that . . .

Lucy Oh, forget it then, if it's so precious. Makes no difference.

Klondike All right then, since you've asked. (*Klondike opens his bag, and reveals the contents, slowly.*)
This is the skin of a poisonous snake,
this is a horse stick, cut from a silver birch,
this is bear's tooth, this is a blue shell,
this is a wren's wing, this is a brass bell,
this is a glass bead, this is a fox tail,
this is a boat, carved from a whale bone,
this is a whistle, this is a goat's horn,
this is driftwood, this is a cat's claw,
this is a ribbon, a mirror, a clay pipe,
this is a toy drum, this is a meteorite,
this is fool's gold, this is buffalo leather –

Lucy All done?

Klondike
And this is the moon and the sun:
a hare's foot and an eagle feather.

Lucy How do you mean?

Klondike That's what they stand for.

Lucy Well, quite a bag full. When's the car-boot sale?

Klondike You couldn't afford them.

Lucy Wouldn't want them. Anyway, what are they for?

Klondike They're just things, that's all.

Lucy Things from a mumbo-jumbo stall?

Klondike Things for dreaming things up.

Lucy What?

Klondike I said, things for dreaming things up.

Lucy Tommy-rot. You're just an overgrown Boy Scout.
  Next thing you'll be showing me a reef knot.

Klondike Get lost, Lucy.

Lucy Dib dib dib, dob dob dob.

Tulip Klondike, show her.

Klondike No.

Tulip Why not?

Lucy Because he can't.

Tulip Show her.

Klondike Why should I?

Lucy Because he's a big kid, playing with toy cars.

Tulip You don't have to take that from her.

Lucy But most of all, because he's full of shite. Eagle
  feathers? Chicken more like.

Klondike All right.

Lucy
  This is the eye of a bat, this is a leprechaun's hat,
  This is the spine of a bird, this is a rocking horse turd –

Klondike I said all right.

Lucy
  This is a snowman's heart, this is a plate of tripe –

Klondike ALL RIGHT. Pick something out.

Lucy Well, well, well. All this for little old me. I don't
  know where to start.

  Eenie, meanie, meinie, mo,

  put the baby on the po . . . no, not my colour.

  Scab and matter custard, toenail pie,
  all mixed up with a dead dog's eye,

31

green and yellow snot cakes
fried in spit,
all washed down with a cup of cold sick.
Here's what I pick.

Klondike The eagle feather.

Lucy None other.

Klondike Put it in the bag, then on the rock, then –

Lucy Let me guess. Light the blue touch and stand well
back?

*Klondike performs a ceremony around the bag. There is
a deafening roar and a brief shadow as a low-flying jet
passes overhead.*

Is that it?

Tulip What?

Lucy Is that it? A jet.

Tulip Oh, only a jet. What do you want, jam on it?
Klondike, you were brilliant. That was the best yet.

Lucy Hang on, let's get this straight. It's the feather that
counts, right? You made that plane come out of the
clouds by doing a voodoo dance around a bit of feather
duster in an old sack?

Klondike Not quite. Something like that.

Lucy Well then, how do you explain . . . this. (*She
produces a rubber duck from the bag.*) Quack quack.

Klondike What . . .

Tulip Where did you get it?

Lucy Down on the beach, washed up. Klondike, say hello
to Mr Duck.

Tulip You're a bitch.

Lucy
Sails on the water, like a cup and saucer. So much for
the jet,
lucky you didn't conjure up the *Titanic*, we might have
got wet.

Tulip I'm going to break her neck.

Klondike No, Tulip.

Lucy Rubber Duck to Ground Control, Rubber Duck to Ground Control, the signal's weak, you're breaking up, you're breaking up.

Tulip You think you're really fucking good, don't you?

Lucy I'm only having some fun. What else is there to do?

Tulip Oh, it's fun, is it? Well, I've had enough. I hope you're either good with a knife, or I hope you can run.

Klondike Tulip, leave her.

Lucy Sorry neither. You'll just have to do me in in cold blood. Mind you, I'm strong.

Tulip Where, apart from your tongue?

Lucy Here, from the shoulder down to the wrist. This right arm doesn't know its own strength.

Tulip Looks to me like a long streak of piss.

Lucy Ah, well, looks deceive. For instance, you don't have to look like a man to be as strong as one.

Tulip And what's that supposed to mean?

Lucy What will you do when your balls drop, Tulip? Grow a beard?

Tulip Right, you're dead.

Klondike Just stop. Knock it off, I said. If you want to show off, why don't you arm-wrestle or something, there on the rock?

Lucy No thanks, I don't play competitive sports.

Klondike Not half you don't.

Tulip Now who's chicken?

Lucy I've told you, I'm just not interested in winning.

Tulip Not interested in losing, more like. Come on, arm-wrestle, or maybe I just smash your face in anyway, for a bit of fun, for a laugh.

Lucy All right, but don't say you didn't ask for it.

Klondike Both of you down on one knee, elbows straight and a clean grip. Ready?

Tulip Yep.

Klondike Lucy?

Lucy As I'll ever be.

Klondike When I say three. One, two –

Enter Midnight, carrying a melting ice-cream in both hands.

Midnight Ice-cream. I got the ice-cream.

Klondike Not now, Midnight.

Midnight 'Greensleeves', up by the road. A screwball, right, and a ninety-nine. Or was it a cone?

Klondike Midnight, we're busy. Just wait there for a minute. And count to three.

Midnight Why?

Klondike Just do it.

Midnight OK then. One. Two. Three.

With her free hand, Lucy takes hold of the electric cable. Tulip is thrown over backwards with the shock.

What was that? Lightning?

Lucy No, something like it. Is she OK?

Klondike Just frightened, I think.

Lucy Ten volts, that's all. Hardly enough to light a torch, but it's the shock I suppose.

Klondike How come?

Lucy Meaning what?

Klondike How come her, and not you?

Lucy Easy. Insulation. Good shoes.

Klondike She was the earth?

Lucy Yes. Here, she can have them back – not my style, rubber boots. (*She takes off the boots and tosses them on the floor.*)

Klondike She was the earth.

Lucy Certainly was.

Klondike Just for a laugh.

Lucy No, self-defence.

Klondike I see. (*He picks up Tulip's knife.*) Well, that's
  enough.

Lucy What do you mean?

Klondike I mean, enough's enough.

Lucy Klondike, that's real. That's a knife.

Klondike That's right. That's right.

Midnight (*facing the opposite way*) Klondike. No heat.

Klondike No heat. Ice-cream. That's right.

Midnight No, no heat, on my face. No . . . no light.

Klondike No light?

Midnight No light. No sun.

Lucy Eclipse.

Klondike Eclipse? ECLIPSE. Everyone into position.
  Who's missing?

Tulip The twins.

Klondike Polly. Jane. POLLY. JANE. How long left?

Tulip A minute. No, fifty seconds. Less.

Klondike Who else? Midnight?

Midnight Here, right next to you.

  Enter Polly and Jane.

Klondike Six of us. Six of us.

Tulip Glue Boy. Where's Glue Boy?

Klondike Where's Glue Boy?

Polly We saw him up by the tents.

Jane Out of his head.

Klondike Idiot. How long left?

Tulip Twenty. Less.

Klondike OK, OK. (*to Lucy*) You. It'll have to be you.

Lucy I'm going back to the . . .

Klondike Stay there and don't move.

Tulip Where shall we stand?

Klondike Don't you remember, the plan? (*He begins to
  move them into position.*) You there, you there, you
  there . . .

Midnight What about me?

35

Klondike You stand here.

Lucy Look, I'm not really sure . . .

Klondike Just stay put. You've had it your own way all afternoon, now let's see what you're made of.

Tulip Ten seconds.

Lucy Huh, me at the back then?

Klondike Pole position. Right where it happens.

Facing towards where the sun grows darker, they stand in a triangular formation, with Tulip, Klondike and Midnight at the front, Polly and Jane behind them, and Lucy at the back.

Polly Look out, here it comes.

Jane (*elated*) Oh yes.

Polly Time for the shades. Time for the shades?

Klondike Yes, the shades. Put them on.

Klondike, Tulip, Polly and Jane put on their protective glasses.

Midnight What?

Polly The specs.

Midnight Oh yes. (*He takes his off.*)

Tulip Five seconds, less. Three. Two. One.

Except for Lucy, they begin the chant.

All
Fallen fruit of burning sun
break the teeth and burn the tongue,

open mouth of the frozen moon
spit the cherry from the stone.

SCENE EIGHT

The police interview room.

Klondike
   Dusk and dawn, like that, in the one afternoon.
   For all the world, this is as much as I know.
   We were standing there watching the most spectacular
      show
   on earth, a beam of light from the bulb
   of the sun, made night through the lens of the moon;
   ninety-three million miles – point-blank range. Strange,
   the moon four hundred times smaller in size,
   the sun four hundred times further away;
   in line, as they were for us for once for a change,
   they're the same size. We were set. We were primed.
   Like the riddle says, what can be seen as clear
   as day, but never be looked in the face? This
   was a chance to stand in a star's shade,
   to catch the sun napping or looking the wrong way –
   the light of all lights, turning a blind eye.
   I'm getting ahead of myself – it's hard to describe.
   When the shadow arrived from the east like a stingray,
   two thousand miles an hour, skimming the sea spray,
   two hundred miles across from fin to fin,
   we felt like a miracle, under its wingspan.
   We said nursery rhymes, like frightened children.
   Midnight bats came out of the sea caves, calling,
   birds in the crags buried down in their breasts
   till morning, crabs came out of holes in the sand
   with eyes on stalks to watch for the tide turning.
   When it was done . . . we looked about, and she'd gone.
   Never thought for a second she might be lost,
   just reckoned she wasn't impressed with planets
   and stars and shadows . . . figured she wasn't fussed.

Thought that she'd taken her lime-green self up top,
sidled away, shuffled off. Came as a big black shock
when they called and said she never showed up.
She wasn't us, although we liked her well enough.
She told us things, showed us stuff. It's almost
as if she did us a good turn by putting us all
on the right track. Sad. And that's the whole story.
I wish I could tell you more but I can't. I'm sorry.

SCENE NINE

*The police waiting-room. Tulip, Polly and Jane, Midnight
and Glue Boy, sitting, waiting. Enter Klondike from
interview room.*

Tulip Well?
Klondike Well what?
Tulip Any problems, or not?
Klondike No, none.
Polly What did you tell them?
Klondike Same as everyone else, I presume.
Jane What do they think?
Klondike How should I know? I'm not a mind-reader.
Tulip Well, I don't care. I don't see what else we're
  supposed to say.
Polly Nor me.
Jane Me neither.
Midnight So we can go home?
Klondike No.
Midnight Why not? We're all done, aren't we?
Glue Boy Except for one.
Midnight Oh yes. Sorry. Forgot.

  Off, a voice calls 'Paul Bond'.

Glue Boy That'll be me then.

Tulip Why are they asking him?

Klondike It's his turn. Everyone has to go in.

Polly Fat load of good that'll be. He can't remember his own name at the best of times.

Jane He was out of his brain that day, weren't you, Glue Boy?

Glue Boy High as a kite. Cloud nine.

Off, a voice calls 'Paul Bond'.

Oh, well. Cheerio.

Klondike Glue Boy?

Glue Boy What?

Klondike Whatever you know, get it straight.

Glue Boy Like you, right?

Klondike Right.

Exit Glue Boy into interview room.

Tulip See the news?

Polly No. In the paper again?

Tulip Yes, and on the telly as well this time.

Midnight *News at Ten*?

Tulip Don't know. I was in bed by then, but I saw it at six on the BBC.

Jane What did it say?

Tulip Said that they'd called off the search. Said they'd had aeroplanes over the sea, locals walking the beach, boats in the bay, dogs in the caves and all that for over a week, but they'd called it a day. Said that she might be thousands of miles away by now.

Polly Anything else. Anything . . . new?

Tulip No. Oh yes, they showed her mum and dad.

Klondike I saw that. Him in the suit, her in the hat, going on and on and on.

Jane How old?

Klondike Don't know, but you could see where she got it from.

Pause.

Tulip They're talking about a reconstruction.

Jane What's one of those when it's at home?

Tulip We all go back to the place and do it again, see if somebody remembers anything or seeing anyone.

Polly And they do it on film, don't they?

Jane Oh yes, and someone'll have to dress up as her, won't they?

Polly With her stuff, and her hair.

Tulip That won't be much fun.

Pause.

Klondike Not a problem. Can't be done.

Midnight You sure.

Klondike Certainly am. Not without the moon, and not without the sun.

Pause.

Tulip Anyway, when's the next one?

Polly Next what?

Tulip Eclipse. Klondike?

Klondike Don't know, I'll have to look at the list. Why, are you up for it?

Tulip Can a duck swim?

Klondike Polly? Jane?

Polly In.

Jane In.

Tulip What about him in there – Mr Pritt-Stick?

Klondike Mr dip-stick more like. Don't worry about him, he'll be all right.

Tulip What about you, Midnight?

Midnight Sorry, I wasn't listening.

Tulip Don't play the innocent with me, sunshine. The next eclipse – yes or no, sir?

Midnight Lunar or solar?

Klondike Solar. Total.
Midnight
> Two days in a van with my mum's barley sugars and the
>   old man.
> Two minutes at most of afternoon night when I'm
>   already blind.
> Hanging around with you lot, calling me names, playing
>   tricks
> of the light and stupid games, then egging myself for a
>   week,
> can't eat, can't sleep, then twenty questions by the
>   police,
> and all the rest, enough to put a normal person in the
>   funny farm
>
> . . . go on then, you've twisted my arm.

SCENE TEN

The police interview room.

Glue Boy
> I suppose you've heard it needle and thread times five.
> Saying it over and over again – not much point, right?
> Any road, I was all of a dither back then,
> disconnected, fuse blown in the head, loose ends,
> nobody home, fumes on the brain – know what I mean?
> Hard to think of it all in one long line, it's all
> squiggles and shapes. Fits and starts. Kills the cells,
> you see, after so long, so that you can't tell. Well,
> nothing to speak of coming to mind just yet. Except . . .
> no, nothing, nothing. All gone funny. Not unless
> you mean the bit between the last bit and the rest?
> You should have said. Let's think. Let's think.
> No point saying it over and over to death, no sense
> wasting breath. Bits and bobs. Chapter and verse.

Unless . . .

no, nothing. What the others said. Just that. Oh yes,
then this . . .

SCENE ELEVEN

The beach. Klondike, Lucy, Tulip and Midnight, as before.

Lucy Klondike, that's real. That's a knife.

Klondike That's right. That's right.

Midnight (*facing the opposite way*) Klondike. No heat.

Klondike No heat. Ice-cream. That's right.

Midnight No, no heat, on my face. No . . . no light.

Klondike No light?

Midnight No light. No sun.

Lucy Eclipse.

Klondike Eclipse? ECLIPSE. Everyone into position.
Who's missing?

Tulip The twins.

Klondike Polly. Jane. POLLY. JANE. How long left?

Tulip A minute. No, fifty seconds. Less.

Klondike Who else? Midnight?

Midnight Here, right next to you.

Enter Polly and Jane.

Klondike Six of us. Six of us.

Tulip Glue Boy. Where's Glue Boy?

Klondike Where's Glue Boy?

Polly We saw him up by the tents.

Jane Out of his head.

Klondike Idiot. How long left?

Tulip Twenty. Less.

Klondike OK, OK. (*to Lucy*) You. It'll have to be you.

Lucy I'm going back to the . . .

Klondike Stay there and don't move.

Tulip Where shall we stand?

Klondike Don't you remember the plan? (*He begins to move them into position.*) You there, you there, you there . . .

Midnight What about me?

Klondike You stand here.

Lucy Look, I'm not really sure . . .

Klondike Just stay put. You've had it your own way all afternoon, now let's see what you're made of.

Tulip Ten seconds.

Lucy Huh, me at the back then?

Klondike Pole position. Right where it happens.

Facing towards where the sun grows darker, they stand in a triangular formation, with Tulip, Klondike and Midnight at the front, Polly and Jane behind them, and Lucy at the back.

Polly Look out, here it comes.

Jane (*elated*) Oh yes.

Polly Time for the shades. Time for the shades?

Klondike Yes, the shades. Put them on.

Klondike, Tulip, Polly and Jane put on their protective glasses.

Midnight What?

Polly The specs.

Midnight Oh yes. (*He takes his off.*)

Tulip Five seconds, less. Three. Two. One.

Except for Lucy, they begin the chant.

All
Fallen fruit of burning sun
break the teeth and burn the tongue,

open mouth of the frozen moon
spit the cherry from the stone.

*Enter Glue Boy from opposite direction, still with glue
bag on his head. He collides with Lucy, who takes him
to one side and takes the bag from his head. She holds
his hands as he hallucinates.*

Glue Boy Seeing things. Dreaming things.

*Glue Boy blurts out his dream as Midnight leaves the
group, retrieves his crucifix from Lucy's bag and puts it on.*

head through a noose dreams
   lasso roping a horse
needle threading itself
   bat flying into a cave
mole coming up through a grave
   cuckoo's head through the shell of an egg
dog on a leash dreams

*Midnight rejoins the group, who are still facing the
eclipse, chanting. Tulip leaves the group and begins
putting on her boots. She also produces another red
headscarf from her pocket, and ties it around her
head.*

sea-horse   trying on its shoes
   tom-cat   tortoiseshell   stood up
mermaid scaling the beach
   finding its feet   ditching its tail
square of the sky   shepherd's delight
   pulled down   worn as a crown
poppy blazing in a field of corn
   dead volcano   blowing its top
matchstick wearing heat to its head like a hat
   dream things   things like that

*Tulip rejoins the group. The twins go to the bag to
retrieve clothes, jewellery and make-up.*

double-vision dream   two trees
   Dutch Elms coming back into leaf
two snow-leopards   trying on furs
   leggings   coats of sheep that were shorn
two African rhino   stripped to the bone
   locking horns
nude Aunt Sally   birthday suit on a tailor's dummy
   rose-petal lips   ivory teeth
dreams   dolled up like Russians
   dressed to the nines   clothes of their mothers
those dreams   others

*The twins rejoin the group. Klondike goes to the bag to
retrieve the skull and the Boji stones.*

nutcracker man coming out of his shell
   great auk treading thin air
phoenix roasting   driftwood fire
   unicorn meeting its match   point of a spear
head of a griffin   worn as a hat
   beak of a dodo worn on a boot
as a spur
   tusk of a mammoth   torn from its root
a tooth   a tree
   white hart hung by its hooves
Franklin's men   out of the deep-freeze
   dream things   those   these

*Lucy and Glue Boy have become stuck together with
the glue. They spin round violently trying to free
themselves of each other.*

Lucy Let go.
Glue Boy It's the glue. It's the glue.
Lucy LET ME GO.

*The rest of the group are still chanting. The total
darkness of the eclipse descends, then sunlight returns,*

*and Glue Boy is found to be standing in the position
where Lucy stood.*

Klondike That's it.
Tulip Blown away.
Polly That was strange. Really strange.
Jane Funny, I've gone all cold.
Midnight I feel sick.
Klondike Happens to some people. I've read about that.
Tulip Come on, everyone up to the top.
Klondike Glue Boy?
Glue Boy Hello.
Klondike Where did she go?
Glue Boy Where did who go?
Tulip Princess Muck. Lady Di. Who do you think? Lucy
  Lime.
Glue Boy Er, don't know. Lost her in the light.
Polly (*picking up Lucy's bag*) She's left her bag.
Jane Here, Glue Boy, better give it her back.

Glue Boy walks off with her bag.

Klondike Come on. We're wasting time.
Jane It seemed to go on for hours. How long did it last?
Tulip Two minutes thirty-five.
Polly Not according to mine. Yours must be fast.
Tulip So what did you make it then?
Polly Well . . . less.
Klondike Come on. Last one to the top gets a Chinese
  burn.
Midnight I feel sick.
Klondike Somebody give him a hand. Polly and Jane.
Tulip Hang on.
Klondike Now what.
Tulip (*looking around*) Nothing. Just checking.

As everyone pauses, Tulip runs on in front of them.

46

Last one up's a chicken!

They all exit, Polly and Jane dragging Midnight with them.

SCENE TWELVE

The interview room. Glue Boy holding Lucy's bag,
examining it.

Glue Boy
Sorry, I just wanted to be sure. Yes, this is the one,
the one that she had on the beach. It's been a bad week.
We're all cracking up with thinking what to think.
We've made up a rhyme to say at the service tonight,
something that fits, we reckon, kind of a wish or prayer
to cover whatever's gone on, wherever she's gone.
I could run through it now, if you like? You'll say
if you think we've got it all wrong? OK then, I will.

As he begins, he is joined in the chanting at various
intervals by the others in the waiting-room.

under the milk token of the moon
under the gold medal of the sun
under the silver foil of the moon
under the Catherine wheel of the sun
born below the sky's ceiling
at home with the moon's meaning
nursed on the dew's damp
twilight for a reading lamp
tribe of the blue yonder
Cub Scouts of Ursa Minor
the east wind for a hair-dryer
Mercury for a shaving mirror
a-bed afoot Jacob's ladder
head down on Jacob's pillow

heaven's sitting tenants
meteorites for birthday presents
Masai of the stone deserts
stage-lit by daffodil heads
Orion's belt for a coat peg
Uranus for an Easter egg
tumbleweed of the world's park
hearers of the world's heart
ears flat to the earth's floor
thawed by the earth's core
needled by Jack Frost
high priests of the long lost
passed over by Mars
pinned down by the North Star
some type of our own kind
branded with real life
Lobby Ludds of the outback
seventh cousins gone walkabout
Navaho of the tarmac plains
snowdrifts for Christmas cakes
groupies of the new age
Venus for a lampshade
Jupiter for a budgie cage
Saturn for a cuckoo clock
guardians of the joke dogs
Jack Russells in tank tops
Sirius for a pitbull
Pluto for a doorbell
Neptune for night-nurse
civilians of the universe
Eskimos of the steel glaciers
St Christopher's poor relations
citizens of the reservations
under the bullet hole of the moon
under the entry wound of the sun
under the glass eye of the moon

under the bloody nose of the sun
under the cue ball of the moon
under the blood orange of the sun
under the sheriff's shield of the moon
under the blowtorch of the sun
under the stalactite of the moon
under the nuclear blast of the sun
under the hammered nail of the moon
under the cockerel's head of the sun
under the iceberg tip of the moon
under the open heart of the sun
under the cyanide pill of the moon
under the screaming mouth of the sun
under the chocolate coin of the moon
under the chocolate coin of the sun

FRIENDLY FIRE

Peter Gill

Characters

Adie

Dumb Dumb

Shelley

Gary

Kenny

Wally

Cheesey

Donna

Karen

A Statue of a Soldier

The play is set around a war memorial,
in a street, Karen's house, a changing room,
Shelley's house, and a field.

The stage is bare. Chairs can be used where necessary.
For example, the changing room can be suggested
by a row of chairs. But apart from the essential
properties, no other representation is required.

The statue is played by an actor. No attempt should
be made to indicate a real statue. This should be effected
by the actor's dress and stance. He should be dressed
in the full battle dress of a private soldier in the
First World War. The pose and look should be suggested
by the statues of Charles Sergeant Jagger, particularly
the Great Western Memorial in Paddington Station.

SCENE ONE

The War Memorial.

Gary, Adie, Cheesey, Dumb Dumb, Kenny and Wally carry the statue onto the bare stage and put it into its position. It is a statue of a young soldier commemorating the First World War. He is reading a letter.

Gary, Cheesey, Wally and Kenny leave Dumb Dumb and Adie on the stage.

Dumb Dumb looks up at the statue. Adie speaks to the audience.

Adie That statue is a memorial statue commemorating the fallen of the First World War. It's Dumb Dumb's favourite statue. It's the only statue he's ever seen, I think. That's Dumb Dumb looking at the statue now. I'm Adie. We go to the same school. (*He leaves the stage.*)

Dumb Dumb (*to the statue*) What does it say? Who's it from? What you reading? Is it from your mum? Who's it from then? Eh? Tell us. Go on. Eh? Go on. Can't, can you? No. You can't.

Adie comes on.

Adie You seen Gary, Dumb Dumb?

Dumb Dumb shakes his head.

You seen Shelley?

Dumb Dumb shakes his head.

53

You ain't seen either of them? I thought I was going to be late. But I'm always on time. Always. But I always think I'm going to be late. How about you?

Why don't you ever say *anything*, eh? I don't know why I'm asking. I don't think I ever heard you speak above a whisper. In class, on occasion, you say something once in a blue moon. If you can be persuaded. If they can be bothered. You do, don't you? You're a chatterbox. Sometimes you are. A right chatterbox. See, you cracked a smile, you did. If you don't say nothing, that's why no one don't bother with you, in it? I've told you. They ain't got time. I got time. That's why I'm bothering. But they don't have time. (*Adie looks at the statue.*) He don't say much either. But then that's how he's made, in it?

(*to the statue*) Is that it? Is that how you're made? Is that it, eh? Are you one of the fallen?

(*to Dumb Dumb*) You're not one of the fallen, though, are you? Eh? You talk too much you do, that's your trouble. Ha ha. No, though. You ought to try more. That's why they picks on you. It's annoying. You know it is. You could be interesting. You could be. You could be East of Eden. You could be cannonball out of the sky. I've heard you speak. You spoke last week when Crackle made you. You did. You said yes or something. You did. (*Indicates the statue.*) Do you like him? I like him. Look at him. Do you like him? My mum says every Christmas Eve he comes alive and goes down Union Street to see his mum. Straight. There's Shelley.

(*to the audience*) There's my friend Shelley. She's late. They're always late. The pair of them. Shelley and my other mate, Gary.

(*to Dumb Dumb*) There's Shelley.

Dumb Dumb Yes.

Adie What?

Dumb Dumb doesn't say anything.

You said something. You did. You did. You wanna watch it. You're a chatterbox.

Shelley comes on.

Hello, Shell. Where you been?
Shelley Sorry.
Adie Dumb's been talking. Ain't you? He's been going on and on. Specially when he seen you, he did. Ain't you?
Shelley Hello, Dumbs.

Dumb Dumb waves and moves off.

Adie That means he's going. Bye.
Shelley Don't laugh at him.
Adie He's not stupid, Shelley. He's not fucking mental. I ain't laughing. Am I? Am I?

Dumb Dumb agrees.

You see.

Dumb Dumb goes.

You seen Gary?
Shelley No, I ain't seen Gary.
Adie Oh dear. Sorry. He's coming out. He said. Where you been then?
Shelley I been down the pet rescue centre.
Adie What you been down there for again? You're always down there. You're getting awful girly, Shelley.
Shelley I'm going there full-time in the summer holidays. Anyway, I'm not always down there, only weekends and the one night. I went in 'cos they got a cat I told them about was neglected.
	Well then, where's Mr Wonderful? Ain't he coming?
Adie He's coming. He's coming.

Shelley Where we going? We going up town?

Adie I don't know. Got any money?

Shelley No.

Adie Gary got money. He'll have money.

Shelley He won't put his hand in his pocket.

Adie He will. What do you say that for?

Shelley He's tight.

Adie He ain't.

Shelley Where we going then?

Adie Down the arcade. Outside Macdonald's. Stand outside places. Look at the pictures outside the pictures. Have some chips. Have a can, one can between three. Have a laugh. We're scallywags, Shell, we are. Go round ours. Or Gary's.

Shelley No, I wanna go up town. I want to look at them jackets.

Adie There's Gary. (*to the audience*) Here's Gary. He's our mate. That makes three. See. Her. Him. And me. (*to Shelley*) There's Gary.

Gary comes on.

Gary (*to Shelley*) I called for you.

Shelley What for?

Adie Where you been?

Gary Where was you?

Adie She been down the pet centre.

Gary You're always down there.

Adie I told her.

Shelley Animals are more worth it than people. Better than most of the people I know. That's true, that is.

Adie See, if you was a dog she'd be nicer to you. If you was a dog. And she's a veggy.

Shelley I always been a vegetarian. Nothing new about that.

Gary Where we going?

Adie Got any money, Gaz?

Gary Not much. Ain't you got none?

Adie No I ain't. Shelley ain't got none neither.

Gary Well, where we going then? There's nowhere to go.

Adie What you got on?

Gary What?

Adie You washed your hair.

Gary Yeah. So?

Adie You're a ponce.

Gary 'Cos I washed my hair? Shelley's washed her hair, haven't you?

Shelley Yeah.

Adie He've got moisturiser on.

Gary You got a necklace on.

Adie Good, in it? Shelley made it.

Gary Let's have a see. (*He examines the necklace.*) Will you make me one of them?

Shelley No. I won't.

Gary Oh.

Adie Go on. Make him one. Go on, he wants one.

Shelley Oh, get the beads then. I'll make you one.

Gary Go round my house?

Shelley No. Up town. I wanna look at them jackets.

Adie Here's the men in black. (*to the audience*) That's Wally and Kenny, that is. Kenny and Wally. They're in our class too. Well, Wally is. Kenny's always on holiday.

Enter Kenny and Wally.

Kenny Hello. Hello.

Wally Where you off?

Adie We're off to see the wizard.

Gary Gis a fag, Shell.

Shelley Honest, Gary.

Gary I'll buy some. I'll buy some.

Wally Where you going?

Shelley You're not coming.

Kenny We're not coming, Wally.

Wally Oh, ain't we? Dear. Dear. That's a bit of a choker.

Kenny Hey, Shell. Karen Loder's had her baby. You heard?

Shelley Oh yeah.

Kenny I thought she was a mate of yours.

Shelley She was.

Kenny Didn't you know?

Shelley 'Course I knew.

Wally Ooo, ooo.

Shelley What?

Kenny Ooo, dear. Fell out, did yer?

Wally Here's Cheesey.

Adie (*to the audience*) Cheesey. Oh dear. He's in our class too.

Gary Cheesey. Oh, blimey. Come on, Adie.

Adie OK.

Enter Cheesey.

Cheesey Hello.

Shelley So long.

Cheesey Where you going?

Wally They're not going anywhere, Cheesey.

Kenny And we're not going anywhere with them, Wally.

Shelley And you ain't coming neither, Cheesey.

Cheesey Shelley, you're a cow.

Kenny It's a hostile world, man. It's a hostile world.

Cheesey I don't wanna go nowhere with them. Where they going anyway?

Kenny They're not going nowhere, Cheesey. Are you, Shelley?

Gary Come on then, Shelley.

Gary, Adie and Shelley leave.

Cheesey Well then, what you two up to then?

Kenny What we up to, Wall?

Wally All sorts, Ken.

Dumb Dumb has come on when Gary, Shelley, and Adie leave.

Cheesey Hey, you. What you looking at – you spas. Go on. Fuck off. Hang round for eh? Well, say something. You're stupid, you are.

Kenny Leave it out Cheesey. What's the matter with you?

Cheesey Yeah. Yeah. What's the matter with you and all?

Cheesey strongarms Kenny.

Kenny Leave off. Don't start.

Cheesey Behave yourself then.

Wally You could be a soccer hooligan, Cheesey, if you wanted to be.

Kenny He is a soccer hooligan. Only he can't get organised.

Wally Only he can't play football.

Kenny Only he don't grasp the offside rule.

Wally Not when he plays, he don't.

Cheesey I ain't no soccer hooligan.

Kenny You are a soccer hooligan, only you ain't been given the chance. Have you, Cheese? If you had the brains you could walk through a storm with your head held high.

Cheesey strongarms him again.

Don't.

Cheesey Well, behave then. Yeah. I'd like to go over there – Italy and that. France, Spain. Few cans. Who? Kick his head in. England. England. Man United – poofs and girls. Ooo, ooo. (*He grunts and kicks an imaginary head in.*) Scum. You Irish scum. England. When my uncle was stabbed, remember, yeah? The geezer only got five years. Five years he got. No fuss then. No enquiry then. No. Then. That's 'cos he was white and because he was English. Not getting off. Hard done by. Not me. I'm different, I am. I'm English. If I was like a cripple, I'd show them. I'd prove that I could walk. I'd prove it to them. No. No. I'll do what I like. Don't stop me. You watch me, I will. England.

(*to Dumb Dumb*) What you laughing at? Don't laugh.

Kenny He ain't laughing. We ain't laughing.

Cheesey Wankers.

He strongarms him.

Kenny Don't.

Cheesey Behave then. Wanker.

Wally They should have that above the blackboard. They should have it above all the blackboards.

Kenny What?

Wally Everybody masturbates.

Cheesey What's that then?

Kenny Yeah? What if you don't masturbate?

Wally Then you're a wanker.

Kenny Are you a wanker, Wall?

Wally Are you, Ken?

Kenny I have a wank but I ain't a wanker, Wall. I bet Dumb Dumb has a sly wank. Don't you, eh? And Cheesey. Well Cheesey. He's a wanker who wanks.

Cheesey Shut up.

Kenny Yes, sir. Yes, sir.

Wally Yes, guv.

Kenny Yes, Your Honour.

Wally Yes, Your Majesty.

Kenny Yes, My Lord.

Wally Yes, mum.

Kenny Yes, Squire.

Wally Yes, cunt.

Kenny Yes, Your Highness.

Wally Yes, love.

Kenny Yes, madam.

Wally Yes, officer.

Kenny Yes, sergeant.

Wally Yes, miss.

Kenny Yes, miss, miss, miss, miss.

Wally Yes, yes. Mum, Mum.

Kenny Yes, yes.

Cheesey You're off it, you two.
        What you gonna do then? Got anything on you?

Wally I ain't got anything.

Kenny Got the makings of a spliff. Is that what you
        want, Cheesey? I ain't got nothing.

Cheesey Where can we get something from? Where can
        we get something to smoke? Get a speed on.

Wally Over Ganga land.

Cheesey I ain't going over there, nigger country. Chasing
        macaroons. That's the other side a town. I'm not
        going all the way over there. And I ain't got no
        money. Got any?

Wally Don't look at me and don't ask Dumb. He's a
        good boy.

Kenny My dad grows it where he lives now.

Wally He don't.

Kenny He do. My dad, not my dad, my dad.

Wally His real dad.

Cheesey He got a real dad?

Kenny Ho ho. He's a traveller.

Cheesey Don't be soft.

Kenny He's with the travelling people. That's why I ain't
        seen him. But I seen him. When I went down there.
        He says school's no good to anyone. No more it ain't.

Wally That's why they've excluded you, Ken. It's not
        good for you.

Kenny I'm a traveller.

Wally You're a time traveller.

Kenny Let's go in the woods. Stop them chopping that copse. That copse. That copse. Burleigh Copse. Sixty odd, hundreds of years old. I'm a travelling man. No. Them roads bad. Protest. No. I'm dangerous. Big man, me.

Cheesey What you on about?

Kenny Tcha.

Wally Chill, man.

Kenny I'm a travelling man. Ooo ooo. On a train. School trip. To the moon. School trip to nowhere. School trip to London. School trip to Edinburgh. School trip to Lego-Land. School trip to Disneyland. School trip to Hell. School trip to dull places. I'm bad. Bad man. My dad. My home dad. He, he says I'm a bad character.

Wally And quite right he is.

Kenny Your mother, Wall.

Wally Your mother, Ken.

Kenny He beats me up 'cos I'm bad.

Wally Well, you are bad.

Cheesey (*to Dumb Dumb*) What you laughing at? Don't laugh.

Kenny He ain't laughing.

Wally Leave it.

Cheesey No.

Kenny Come on.

Cheesey No.

　　　(*to Dumb Dumb*) What you laughing at? Say something. Go on.

Wally He's not speaking.

Kenny He don't have nothing to say.

Cheesey Say something, go on.

Dumb Dumb moves away.

Where you going? Let's do him. He annoys me. Don't go. Where you going? You're annoying me.

He hurts Dumb Dumb.

Dumb Dumb Nowhere.
Cheesey See, it speaks. You're a freak. Let's do him. Let's strip him. Get something to tie him up.
Kenny No.
Wally Come on. Let's go.
Cheesey (*to Dumb Dumb*) How much you got on you, eh?
Wally Come on.
Cheesey Eh? Punch him, go on.
Kenny No.
Wally I'm going.
Cheesey Go on.
Kenny No. Don't be stupid.

Kenny and Wally go.

Cheesey Scum. Dumb. Ain't you got anything? Eh? I'll have that though.

He takes a chocolate bar from Dumb Dumb.

Ooo. Crunchy. Thanks.

He twists his arm.

Don't talk to me, then. (*He points to the statue.*) Talk to him.

SCENE TWO

Karen's house.
  Donna is holding Karen's baby.

Adie (*to the audience*) This is Karen's house. That's
  Donna holding Karen's baby. Karen's in our class and
  Donna is too. Only we don't know if Karen's coming
  back. It's a nice house. Her mum keeps it nice.
  Council do it up every seven years. (*She goes.*)
Donna In she lovely?
Karen Don't wake her.
Donna I won't.
Karen Put her down, Donna.
Donna In a minute. In she lovely? Don't you wanna pick
  her up all the time?
Karen No. I don't. She ain't a doll. Get enough of that
  at night.
Donna In she gorgeous?
Karen Yeah. I know.

  Donna puts the baby down.

Donna There we are, darling.
  Do you wanna fag?
Karen Don't smoke. Give it up. Not good for the baby.

  Donna lights up.

Don't smoke all over her.
Donna I won't.
  When you coming back to school?
Karen I don't know.
Donna You're coming back though?
Karen Not yet.
Donna But you're coming back?
Karen Yeah. I am.

Donna How you gonna manage?

Karen I'll manage. My mum's giving up work.

Donna You still look tired, Karen.

Karen I am.

Donna You gotta look after yourself.
    She get through the night yet?

Karen No. I been crying a lot. You cry easy. I get tired.
    She'll wake in a minute. You see. I've got a bottle
    made up.

Donna Why, ain't you breast feeding her?

Karen No. I don't want to. I did in the hospital. I ain't
    got the patience now.

Donna What you calling her?

Karen I don't know yet. My mum wanted to call her
    Diana and my Aunty Gloria. But my dad said it was
    morbid.

Donna Lucky she wasn't a boy. They might have wanted
    you to call her Dodi. Diana would have been nice
    though.

Karen I know. I'd like to call her Danielle after Danny.

Donna You heard from him?

Karen Yeah. Letter there. Read it if you like.

Donna Thanks. Diana would have been nice, though.

Karen Yeah. Poor cow.

Donna She was done in, Diana. Definite. Murdered, she
    was. The Queen and the Secret Service had her done
    in. They put a contract out on her. They couldn't risk
    it, she was going to marry Dodi. She was pregnant.
    They couldn't have a Muslim and that. They had it
    done.

Karen No, that's not right. I don't believe that. My
    mother says she was seen leaving the tunnel. This
    woman in the flats nearby saw a woman in white
    leave the tunnel. She walked away. Then she done a
    runner. They had it all planned. She's living in
    America. Wills and Harry, Wills he's called, they

know. So they're alright. They know, of course. My Aunty Gloria knows all about everything about Diana. She've got pictures, she've got books, she've got mugs, she've got plates, she've got a Diana doll from America. Says she's keeping it for the baby. She knows all about it. Or they say she went up in a spaceship. They come for her. She blames the Queen Mum. She says she's an evil bitch. She says they ruined that other poor cow's life.

Donna Who?

Karen Princess Margaret.

Donna In she dead?

Karen No, she lives in Jamaica.

Donna Diana was only ordinary, see. She was only a nanny. They saw her off. My grandmother says she was more upset over that than when my grandfather died.

Karen My granddad says shoot the lot. He wouldn't have them on the telly. Only he don't have no say in our house. Go home my mother says. He goes mad. He goes around muttering.

Donna You couldn't call a baby Camilla, could you?

Karen No. Not now you couldn't.

Donna Nice name, though. (*indicating the letter*) It's a lovely letter. I thought your mum didn't want you to see him no more, Danny.

Karen I know. She don't like him. I don't see him much anyway. Now he's on remand. Visits. He's gonna phone later. They can on remand.

Donna Why don't she like him? Too much of the smokey and the cokey?

Karen Well, I've always been a bit of a rebel. That's me. They throw a brick. I throw one back.

Donna (*reading the letter*) 'I'll stand by you, Karen.' That's nice.

66

Karen He's worried about his dog though.

Donna Why?

Karen Well, his mum's got it. She don't want to keep it. I can't have it here. My mum won't have it anyway. He got no friends, here.

Donna What?

Karen Well, he got other dogs there. Splash, he's called.

Donna Ask Shelley. She knows all about what to do with dogs and that.

Karen No. I'm not speaking to her. She thinks she's someone.

Donna You fall out? I've heard you're not speaking.

Karen I can't be asked. She never asks me round her house. She's always round here. I can't be asked. Shirley Thomas asked for her phone number. I rang her up from the hospital.

Donna Didn't she visit you?

Karen Oh yes. I said is it alright to give her your phone number? I'm not going round giving out phone numbers. She thought it was funny. I had a pair of shoes off of her for £15. The day I gave her the money I could see she was ready to have a go in case I never paid her. I can't be asked. She can be a very selfish person. But that's me, see. This is me and I ain't gonna change for no one. This is me. I don't want no false friends. They're no use to you. Gis a drag. (*Draws on cigarette.*) And she said things behind my back. Like, I was stupid and that, why didn't I take precautions.

Donna Oh!

Karen Anyway I think it was up to Danny. He said he was being careful and that.

Donna Don't you take the pill?

Karen No I don't. I don't take no pill.

Donna She was a good mate.

Karen I know. We was good mates. But we wasn't the fucking Supremes though, was we? She hangs round with that Adie, anyway, don't she.

Donna I fancy him.

Karen And Gary.

Donna You used to like him.

Karen She goes round with them, anyway. They're weird.

Donna We used to have laughs. In the field, remember? Where there was a big dip, where there was a bomb crater – from the Second World War. Where we used to make fires, throw aerosol cans.

Karen That one blew up.

Donna That was you.

Karen Singed all my hair. Coppers thought it was the bomb.

Donna I gotta go. (*She sneezes.*)

Karen What's the matter?

Donna I always get a summer cold.

Karen That's pollen, that is.

Donna Ooo, I forgot. I brought you this. (*Gives her a matinee jacket.*) My mum had it made.

Karen Oh, it's lovely.

Donna See you. When can you come out? Can you?

Karen I can come out. I can't stay in for ever, can I?

Donna Oh, we'll go out then.

Karen Not Shelley.

Donna No. Tara then. She's a lovely baby.

SCENE THREE

The street.

Adie (*to the audience*) We're up town. We been everywhere. She seen the jackets. She don't like 'em. Gary's gone to get us a drink.

Gary carries on two drinks.

Gary Here you are.

He gives Adie a drink.

Shelley Did you get me one?
Gary You said you didn't want one. I asked you.
Shelley I didn't.
Gary You did, Shelley. I said special. Did you want one?
Shelley I said after. Didn't I?
Gary Did she?
Adie Yeah. She did. She called after you.
    I'll get her one.
Gary No. I'll get her one. (*to Shelley*) Anyway, here's
    your fags. (*Gives her fags.*) You alright for a bit?
Shelley Don't bother.
Gary No, I'll get you one.
Adie You two. You two. Honest. Stop it. What's the
    matter with you? You got to stop this.
Gary You're bad tempered, Shelley. You're a difficult
    woman. She's moody, isn't she? Moody cow. (*He goes
    to get another drink.*)
Adie Why you so angry with him, Shell? You know
    what he's like about you.
Shelley That's not my fault.
Adie You used to like him.
Shelley I never. Not . . . I can't help it. Like you can't
    help it. Why did all this have to happen? We was OK.
Adie What?
Shelley You know what. Now he won't leave me alone.
    I can't help it any more than you. Anyway he likes you
    more than he likes me. It's just sex. He do. He do. He
    likes you more than you like him, only you can't see it.
Adie Behave yourself.
Shelley I'll do what I like. I know nothing won't work
    out, though. Will it?

Adie What?

Shelley Nothing. Have you seen Karen Loder's baby?

Adie I haven't.

Shelley Her baby? I have. She won't look after a baby. She'll say she will. She won't care for it. Poor babies. All these babies. I don't want a baby.

Adie Don't have a baby.

Shelley They do. They make you decide to have a baby. You have to decide, it's all a big thing, you have to plan. I don't want to have to decide. Karen Loder didn't decide. They make you make decisions. If you don't have a baby, well. Everyone has a baby. They don't do it with boys. You don't have to think.

Do you fancy him? Do you love him?

Adie Fuck off.

Shelley You in love with him?

Adie Don't, Shell.

Shelley Anyway. I know you are. He knows you are. He wouldn't know what to do without you. He wouldn't.

Adie What's he done to you? He's gone to get you a drink. He runs round after you.

Shelley Why when boys do something are they always so pleased with themselves? They always got to get noticed for it. You flatter him. You do. He likes you to flatter him. You do. Just the way you takes notice of him. He loves it. You can't wake boys up and when you do, you can't stop 'em. Like they're out of control. They're always so cool until something affects them, like a football match, or they got a mark on their clean shirt. Then they turn into old women. He's an old woman. He's vain.

Adie Don't you find them, like, well, sweet?

Shelley No, I don't. Look at them when they're doing press-ups. That's the only time they're awake, when they're playing the fool. Times like that. 'Come on.

Come on. You can do it. Once more. And another one my son.'

Adie I like it when they're intent. Don't you see the beauty of him when he's doing something? That's when they become all interested and focused, attentive, surprised. When they're doing something. I like watching him mend his bike. His hands. Have you noticed his hands? Don't matter.

Shelley Where you going?

Adie It's alright. It's alright. (*He goes off.*)

Shelley Adie.

Enter Gary with Shelley's drink.

Gary Where's Adie?

Shelley He's gone.

Gary He'll be back.

Shelley How do you know?

Gary Here's your drink.
    Don't you like me no more?

Shelley Give over, Gary.

Gary What you so narked for? What I do?

Shelley You ain't done nothing.

Gary I have – haven't I?

Shelley You ain't. Don't start moaning.

Gary Why won't you go out with me?

Shelley I am.

Gary No. Don't. Come on.

Shelley I don't go out with no one.

Gary What's the matter with you?

Shelley I don't want your big paws all over me. Alright?

Gary Come on.

Shelley No, get off, Gary. Go after someone else. Go after Donna, or Karen Loder. She's mad about you. Keep your hands off me, Gary.

Gary I'm used to birds following me. What's the matter with you?

Shelley Yeah, well. I'm not following you.

Gary Who do you fancy then?

Shelley I don't fancy no one.

Gary Do you fancy Adie?

Shelley Why can't you shut up?

Gary Sorry. I like you, Shell.

Shelley I like you. You're a mate.

Gary Bloody Adie.

Shelley You like Adie. He's all over you.

Gary Is that why you hang round with us. Adie?

Shelley I don't hang round with no one. What do you mean? We've always hung round together anyway.

Gary You want some big flash bloke, then. Is that it? You waiting for someone who's older, like Karen? You're a snob.

Shelley I ain't. And look what happened to Karen. I can be a friend.

Gary I don't want a friend. I got a friend. I want a girlfriend. I got loads of friends.

Shelley I like you. You know, Gary.

Gary You makes a fool of me. You do. You leads me on.

Shelley I don't.

Gary You do. You do. You know you do. You know what you did.

Shelley You just want to get it on with me. Not me. You're not interested in me. Me.

Gary What do you mean? What do you want?

Shelley I don't want nothing off you.

Gary I'd worship you. I'd look after you.

Shelley I can look after myself. And you wouldn't.

Gary You can't say that.

Shelley You wouldn't. You're only talking about sex.

Gary You look down on people.

Shelley I don't. You and Adie do. You think you're clever. Oh, stop it. What's going on? There used to be just us. Not all this on top of it. Where's Adie?

Gary Adie. Adie. Don't go on about Adie.

Shelley Well, you're all Adie. You can't talk to no one else.

Gary I'm talking to you.

Shelley You're not talking to me.

Gary What you want to talk about then? Eh? Go on. Fuck off.

Shelley You don't have to be like that. Alright, be like that then. Who do you think you are? You can't get what you want, you're in a strop.

Gary I got feelings. Go on. Fuck off.

Shelley I will. (*She goes off.*)

Gary (*shouts after her*) What'll I tell Adie?

Shelley I don't care what you tell Adie.

Enter Adie.

Adie Where's Shelley?

Gary Gone.

Adie Where's she gone?

Gary I don't know and I don't care. She can go where she likes. I don't care. I can get a bird. She won't have me, so what? Fuck it. I feel . . . Fuck it.

Adie What?

Gary I can't do nothing about nothing. Here or in the world. I like being in control. I'm not in control of nothing. I want power. I want to be in charge of nothing more like. We can do nothing. We know we can't. I can't do nothing. What can we do?

Adie You're just angry.

Gary I can't do anything. What can we do? You got no joy of doing anything. Don't matter what I think. Don't matter, except for trainers. Except for can I have a mountain bike, Mum? You know, you're like that. No choice. No choice.

Adie You never know what might happen.

Gary I know what's going to happen. I know what's
going to happen. Nothing. Nowt. Turn you down.
Failed. Not picked for the seven-a-side. We're left out,
let down. Impotent. Get it up where? Cold water.
Drenched, pouring down. I'm not kicking in. Fuck up.
No marks. Doing my very best. Could try harder. I'm
not an individual. I don't want to be an individual.
Sometimes I'm me. Sometimes I'm you. Sometimes I'm
from our street. Sometimes I'm in the pictures.
Sometimes, sometimes, I don't know what they want,
sometimes, sometimes I'm a prisoner. Sometimes I'm
in school. Sometimes I'm in England. Sometimes I'm
in Britain. Sometimes I'm a girl. Sometimes I'm a boy.
Sometimes.

    I want to be in extreme situations. I want to be in
the condemned cell or I want to be in the gas chamber.
Beetle just off mother. I can't control thoughts or
think. Can't have no control over thoughts. Thinking.
Everyone seems to be trapped in the wrong bodies,
in the wrong place, in the wrong person. The wrong
house. Trapped in the wrong house. I've taken my
pictures down off my wall.

    I think at night in the dark, looking out the window
at all the houses that someone's going to turn it off.
Turn it off or on. It's not real. I think I'm in someone's
argument. I cannot believe I exist. I cannot believe
that it's all happening. I think that it's going to be
switched off. How can you bear to have to live? I live
in a TV set. I think of dying. How can we die,
anyway? I wish my mother was dead.

Adie What you say that for? What's the matter with
you?

Gary I want to die. That's all she says. Turn it off. Then
there wouldn't be nothing.

Adie You does too much E, mate. You do.

Gary I don't. Anyway, it don't do you no more harm than traffic. When I last take E? You knows everything I do. I was with you. Months. Safe sex and drugs, that's all you hear. I've had earfuls of it. (*Takes out a condom.*) Look, it's perished. Past its sell by date.

Adie Don't, Gaz.

Gary Look, I want a shag. I only got it for Shelley. For Roger Jenkin's party.

Adie Did you?

Gary You know very well I didn't. What you talking about? You know, Adie. You know I didn't. She don't. Kissed her and then pushed up her mini skirt. Snogged her. Never shagged her. I pushed her mini skirt up. (*He laughs.*)

Adie What you laughing at?

Gary I'm laughing all the way to a wank. She let you?

Adie No, don't.

Gary You seen her fanny?

Adie When we was about six. And you did. And when we went in the sea that night. Put it away. I don't like looking at it. I don't like looking at packets of rubber johnnies in the chemist.

Gary No?

Adie No.

Gary Shy. Scared?

Adie I thought so but no.

Gary Look. (*Shows him the condom.*)

Adie No. I don't like it.

Gary Shy. Scared.

Adie Yeah. Scared you're going to use it.

Gary I will use it. If not this, another one.

Adie I know.

Gary Are women heterosexual? I bet they are. They sound as if they are. What's a typical heterosexual?

Adie Mr Watkins.

Gary No. Brad Pitt. Sylvester Stallone.

Adie Tony Blair, more like.

Gary Mr Dorkin, more like.

Adie More like my dad.

Gary More like Chris de Burgh.

Adie More like.

Gary More like.

Have you got to beat girls up? If you hit her, like, would you hit her like you hit a boy?

Adie I don't know. My father chased my mother up the stairs and she hid in the front bedroom.

Gary I mean. Would you go bang? I'd hit the wall. I'm going to hit the wall. I wouldn't want to do it, hit a girl. I'd like to hit my mother. Do you, like, smash 'em? I'm worried about it. I'm worried all the time.

Adie Worry. Everyone worries, don't they? I worry about everything.

Gary Yes. Well, you're a worrier.

Adie Well, it's life, isn't it?

Gary Why? I'm going to do the hard stuff. I am. I can't be worrying.

Adie You're not.

Gary I'm not. I'm not. Goody goody. I'm not. I might. But I wouldn't.

Adie I'm not goody goody. Shut up Gary.

Gary No. You're my friend. My mate. You're my only one friend I've got. You can't do no wrong. Don't laugh. Don't laugh. She fancies you. She loves you. She does. Why not me? I'm sorry when I take it out on you.

Adie I've had a time you're just having now.

Gary I want love. Why can't I have love then?

Adie Oh. (*He moves away.*)

Gary Do you know what I'm saying? No. You know what I mean. I'd do anything for her if she loved me. The bitch.

Adie Where you going?

Gary I dunno, Adie. Leave me alone. Don't follow me about, Adie.

SCENE FOUR

The War Memorial. The boys bring on the statue.

Adie (*to the audience*) Back to Dumb Dumb's statue. And Kenny and Wally and Donna and Karen. And, yeah, Cheesey, yeah. (*He goes off.*)

Kenny You alright, Wall?

Wally I'm alright, Ken.

Kenny How are you doing?

Wally How many cans you had?

Kenny How many you had?

Wally I've had many cans.

Kenny How are you doing?

Wally I'm alright.

Kenny No, no. You're not. You're nothing, mate. You're scum. Official.

Wally You're right. You're right.

Kenny Trash. Trash.

Donna and Karen come on giggling.

Karen Where are you? Kenny, Kenny?

Kenny Here they are.

Wally Where you been?

Donna Having a wee.

Karen Behind a bush.

Donna Sh. Sh. Don't tell everyone.

Kenny Ladies. Ladies.

Karen Shut up, Kenny.

Enter Cheesey, doing his flies up.

77

I've had a laugh tonight.

Donna And me.

Cheesey Where we going now?

Kenny Here. We're going here.

The girls laugh.

Cheesey Ha ha.

Kenny I'm a bit . . . Ooo . . .

Wally You OK, Kenny?

Kenny I'm OK.

Wally So, you're OK.

Kenny Are you OK?

Wally I'm very OK, thank you, Kenny.

Karen Girl power.

Donna Yeah.

Kenny I got her knickers in my pocket.

Wally You ain't.

Kenny The boy is good. (*showing a pair of knickers*)
These yours, Karen? Are they?

Cheesey Are they, Karen?

Karen They are not. They're not. I got my knickers on.
Look.

She shows them. Boys hoot.

They must be Donna's.

Donna They are not. Look.

Shows her knickers. Hoots from the others.

Cheesey Whose are they then?

Kenny That's how you get girls to show you their
knickers. (*Puts them on his head.*)

Wally Don't put 'em on your head.

Kenny I always put them on my head, Wally. You know
that. (*He wears them for the rest of the scene.*)

Karen Where you get them? You got 'em off our line.
You perve, Kenny. I can't stop laughing. This is my

first time out on my own. It is. It's funny. I ought to go home.

Kenny No, don't go home.

Donna I'll come with you, Karen, in a little while. Stay out a bit longer.

Karen I can't.

Donna Why you crying?

Karen I got to go home. Danny's going to phone. His case is up in court next week.

Donna When?

Karen Next week.

Donna You goin' to court?

Karen Yeah. I got to stand by him. Ain't I?

Donna You going to court?

Karen Yeah. I am.

Donna What about your mum?

Karen I know.

Kenny Come on. Come, Karen. Cheer up.

Cheesey Where we going?

Karen I got to go home.

Dumb Dumb comes.

Donna Look who's here.

Cheesey What you doing here? What you want?

Donna Oh, he's stupid, he is. Leave him. Shoo, stupid. Go on. Go on.

Cheesey Yeah. Go on.

Kenny Leave him.

Donna He gets on my nerves. You do.

Kenny Come on, let's go. Wall?

Wally Yeah, let's go. Leave him alone.

Cheesey No. Let's get him.

Grabs him. Dumb Dumb escapes.

Donna He's escaped.

They chase Dumb Dumb around the stage until they catch him.

Cheesey Ho ho.
Donna You're stupid, you are.
Cheesey Say fucking something. He does sometimes.
Kenny Don't.
Donna Yeah.
Cheesey Say something.
Karen I want to go home.
Donna Make him say something.
Cheesey You want to get him to talk, like? I will. I will. My pleasure.

He twists Dumb Dumb's arm until he calls out.

Kenny Leave off, Cheesey.
Wally Come on, you two.
Donna Yeah, he's stupid.
Cheesey He's nothing. Are you? You're nothing.

Spits at him. Donna laughs.

Karen Come on. I'm going home. Danny might phone.
Cheesey Dumb Dumb, what you got to say? What you got to say? What you got to say? You're a fucking little wanker. You're a fucking little twister, you are.
Kenny Don't. What you doing?
Cheesey It's his fault. He should speak up. He's stupid. You're stupid, are you stupid? What's the matter with you? A little scared? You should be. What's the matter with you? Eh? What's the matter?

Enter Shelley.

Shelley Hey, you. Leave him. Hey. Leave him.
Cheesey (*to Shelley*) You shut up and all.
Kenny Come on, Cheesey.
Cheesey You shut up, Shelley.

Shelley What you doing to him?
Donna Go on, Cheesey.
Shelley I'll have your fucking head off.
Donna Ooo ooo.
Shelley And yours, Donna.
Cheesey Will you?
Shelley (*to Karen*) And yours.
Kenny You alright, Shell?
Wally OK, Shell?
Kenny It's alright, Shell. It's alright.
Cheesey Will you?
Wally Peace, love.
Cheesey Come on then.
Shelley (*to Karen*) You, what you looking at? I'll have you and all . . . I'll have the two of you.
Karen Yeah, will you? Why ain't I home with my baby? Is that it, Shelley?
Shelley That's your business. You said it.
Karen I'll kill her.
Shelley Will you? You won't. You won't.
Kenny See what you done, Cheesey.
Cheesey What? What?

Enter Adie.

Adie You alright, Shelley? What's the matter?
Karen Oh, here's her boyfriend.
Shelley You OK, Dumb Dumb?
Donna Oh Adie.
Shelley Shut up, you.
Karen You just think I'm a fucking Sharon, Shelley.
Adie Well, you are a Sharon, Karen. That's why you're called Karen. 'Cos you're a Sharon.
Kenny Come on.
Wally Come on. We'll buy you a coke.
Kenny Come on, Cheesey.

81

Cheesey Do you want me to do him? Eh? Come here then.

Enter Gary.

Donna Here's her big boyfriend.

Gary Alright, everybody. Are you, are you alright, Cheesey?

Karen Come on. Let's go, Donna.

Kenny Yeah. Come, come on. And you, Cheesey.

Karen Come on Donna. I'm never going to speak to you ever again, Shelley. Come on, Donna.

They exit.

Adie He's the cavalry.

Shelley We'd have managed.

Gary Oh thanks, Shelley.

SCENE FIVE

The changing room.
  Gary, Adie, Cheesey, Wally and Kenny have been playing football and have nearly finished changing and packing their kit.

Adie (*to the audience*) This is the changing room. We been playing football. It was a draw.

Kenny Can I put these in your bag?

Wally Where's my shoe?

Cheesey England. England.

Wally Why didn't you bring your own bag, Kenny?

Kenny Well, Wall. Can I have your foot powder? My mum always gives me a wet towel.

Wally Here.

Cheesey That was never a penalty.

Wally Shut up, Cheesey.

Kenny I'm good looking. I am. Gis your comb.

Wally Ain't you got nothing? Do you want my gel?

Kenny No thanks, Wall.

Cheesey Ooo, ooo.

Kenny Mohicans are back in.

Wally They never was out.

Adie (*to Gary, asking for a comb*) Can I have that?

Wally Not with Mohicans.

Adie Thanks.

Cheesey We was playing against twelve men.

Wally The ref was Mr Dorkin, Cheesey. Spas.

Cheesey That was never a penalty.

Wally Where's the ball?

Kenny I don't know, where is it?

Wally We'd better lock it up. Where is it?

Kenny I dunno.

Wally Oh, yeah. I know. You said you'd had your belly
button pierced.

Kenny I have. You don't wear a ring in a match.

Wally You ain't had it done.

Kenny I have. I ain't going in the shower with you
again, Wally. You got an offensive weapon.

Wally I'm going to have it reduced.

Cheesey I'm not going in the shower with Adie again.
I might drop the soap. Ooops.

Gary Shut up, Cheesey.

Cheesey Oh, Gary, you spoke. They're quiet, the
lovebirds.

Gary Shut up.

Cheesey (*calling off*) See you, Lenny. That was a
cracking goal. Catch you up.

Wally Theirs was a good goal. Wan' it?

Kenny Yeah.

Cheesey What, that schwarzer? No. Rubbish.

Wally Yeah. But that was never offside.

Kenny It was.

Wally No, no.

Kenny It was, Wall.

Cheesey (*calling off*) Hey, Skikey. I'll see you over
there. OK?
    We should have slaughtered them.

Kenny You're quiet, Gary.

Gary I am.

Kenny What's the matter?

Gary Nothing's the matter with me.

Kenny Ooo, dear.

Cheesey Girls. Girls.

Wally I'm starving.

Kenny We going for a burger?

Wally No, I'm going home for tea.

Kenny My mum give me the money for a burger.

Wally You're deprived.

Kenny I know. Someone should make a programme
about me.

Wally They should.

Kenny No. She was being nice. Or a take-away.

Wally Come round our house. Save the money.

Kenny Or have a burger and then go round your house
for tea as well, Wall.

Wally You ought to eat more fruit, that's my mum.

Kenny My shin.

Cheesey Are we playing soggy biscuit?

Wally Shut up.

Kenny Did you hear him?

Wally Cheesey's the only one who's ever eat the soggy
biscuit.

Cheesey I never.

Wally You did.

Kenny No one's ever eat the soggy biscuit.

Wally Cheesey have. He have.

Cheesey Shut up.

Kenny Cheesey, you're a youth.

Cheesey Why are them two so quiet? Why's he so quiet? Why you so quiet?

Kenny He's angry with Adie over Shelley. She won't go out with him.

Cheesey Ooo, lover boy.

Kenny She loves Adie.

Cheesey Won't do her much good. Will it, Gaz?

Gary No, it won't.

Kenny What?

Gary I said it won't. Will it, Adie?

Cheesey Ooo. Sparring up. Is he a bender then? Really? Are you, Adie? Is he?

Gary Yes. She's never going to get him.

Cheesey Is he?

Gary Yes. He wants to suck my cock. Queer cunt.

Adie leaves.

Wally Well?

Kenny Wall.

Adie comes back for his bag.

Cheesey Adie forgot his handbag.

Adie Fuck off.

Adie punches Gary. They fight.

Cheesey Fight, fight.

The others part them.

Kenny Come on.

Wally Come on, Gaz.

Cheesey Come on, Gaz.

Wally There's the ball. Lock it up.

Kenny No. To me.

They play with the ball.

What about him?

Wally He'll be alright. Come on. Leave him.

They leave Adie.

SCENE SIX

Karen's house.
  Karen is giving the baby a bottle. Donna is smoking.

Adie (*to the audience*) Karen's house. She's having
  trouble with her mum. (*He goes.*)

Karen (*calling off*) Mum.

Donna You're never going to court.

Karen (*calling off*) I am. 'Course I am. Who's going to
  stop me?
       Mum. Donna's here. Donna, Donna!
       (*to Donna*) Do you wanna cup of tea?

Donna (*calling off*) Yes. Thank you, Mrs Loder.

Karen I gotta go. He's relying on me. I gotta be there
  when he's in court, haven't I?

Donna But your mum don't want you to go.

Karen I can't help that.
       (*calling off*) Can I have one too, Mum? What? I am
  going, Mum. I am. I am. And I can wear what I like.
  I can. What do you mean, I'll end up with my throat
  cut in a ditch? I'm going. Mum. He might be put
  away. I got to go. What, what?
       (*to Donna*) How many sugars?

Donna Two, please.

Karen I'm going anyway.
       (*to Donna*) How many sugars?

Donna (*calling*) Two please, Mrs Loder.

SCENE SEVEN

Shelley's house.
  Gary comes in to see Shelley.

Adie (*to the audience*) Gary goes to see Shelley in her
  house. (*He goes.*)
Shelley What do you want, Gary? I'm doing something.
Gary What you doing?
Shelley What do you want to know for?
Gary Alright, alright.
    I ain't seen you, have I?
Shelley I got a lot on my mind. I got other fish.
Gary Oh, yeah?
    Seen Adie?
Shelley I seen Adie. I don't know what happened. So
  don't tell me. I don't want to know. I had to shut
  Cheesey up.
Gary I haven't seen Adie.
Shelley Haven't you?
Gary I don't know. What am I supposed to do?
Shelley Nothing as far as I'm concerned, Gary.
Gary I want to see Adie.
Shelley See him.
Gary I can't. Will you see him?
Shelley I seen him.
Gary Will you speak to him for me? Say, you know . . .
  You can do it, Shell. Though he can fuck off if he's
  going to be like that, going to sulk much longer.
Shelley You speak to him.
Gary He won't speak to me.
Shelley Have you tried? You haven't tried.
Gary No. I can't do that.
Shelley Why not?

Gary No. Don't be daft. I can't go running after Adie.
I can't do that.

Shelley Why can't you?

Gary No. You go round, Shell.

Shelley No, you go round. Go on.

Gary Shell . . . Shell.

Shelley Yeah?

Gary I still want you to go out with me.

Shelley Gary. This is daft. What's the matter with you?

Gary You love Adie, don't you? That's it, see. He got
you.

Shelley Shut up, Gary.

Gary Adie likes you.

Shelley Yeah.

Gary You gets on with Adie, like, you gets on with him.
He'll listen to you.

Shelley So what?

Gary What am I going to do?

Shelley Don't ask me.

Gary I wants to talk to Adie.

Shelley Talk to him.

Gary No, no. Anyway, I don't care, see. You can fuck
off, you can. I can do without you and Adie and
anyone and him. You're a bitch, Shelley. I'm going
mad in my head.

Shelley See, you can't get what you want.

Gary No, I can't. Clever, ain't you? Fuck off, I'm in hell
here. In my head. I can't do it. I can't. I'm going.

Shelley Go then. I never asked you to come round.

Gary You're a hard bitch.

Shelley Am I?

Gary It's all since Roger Jenkin's party. I know innit?
That's it.

Shelley What you mean?

Gary It is. First you wanted to come upstairs. Then Adie
don't like it. Then you wouldn't. Then you did. Then

Adie does one. It was all that night. That night when it went all over the fucking place. You fancies Adie. You won't say it though.

Shelley That's my business. Isn't it?

Gary Fuck off then, Shelley. See, I can do without anybody. I can.

SCENE EIGHT

A field.

Gary is sitting down. Adie comes on and talks to the audience.

Adie This is the field near Karen's house where we used to spend a lot of time. There's only a scrappy bit of it left now. I've come looking for Gary.

(*to Gary*) You're here then.

Gary Go away, Adie. No don't, Ade. Don't, Ade. Don't, Ade. Don't go.

Adie I wasn't gonna go.

Gary I'm sorry. I am. I was angry with you. Scared. Wanted to get you. I'm ashamed. My mum wants to know why you ain't been round.

Adie I seen your mum.

Gary When?

Adie Just now. Give us.

Gary What?

Adie Give us, Gary.

Gary What?

Adie Give 'em us.

Gary What's this?

Adie Give 'em us. (*Takes a bottle of pills from Gary's pocket.*)

What you got these for?

Gary I dunno.

Adie You wasn't gonna take them?

Gary I dunno. Ain't many in there.

Adie Enough to do you no good. You took 'em out of your mum's bag – what's the matter with you?

Gary I dunno.

Adie What's the matter?

Gary I would have come to see you.

Adie Not if you took these.

Gary I wasn't going to take them.

Adie Why didn't you come then?

Gary I would have.

Adie Yeah? No, you wouldn't.

Gary I would. I would. You're always first. You can't wait for nothing.

Adie I can't wait for nothing, only you. You can't wait for nothing that you really want. Like Shelley.

Gary That's no good.

Adie What we going to do?

Gary I don't know. I don't know what we going to do. We used to play about, like. Didn't we? We did, Adie.

Adie I know. I know. What do you want to do?

Gary I dunno.

Adie Do you want to?

Gary No. No thanks. I couldn't.

Adie You want everything, you do.

Gary I don't.

Adie You want Shelley.

Gary It's only natural, isn't it?

Adie Oh, aye.

Gary Shelley, she's a tease.

Adie She's not.

Gary She can have it.

Adie She don't want it.

Gary She ain't going to get it.

Adie You're afraid when you ain't got power.

Gary You took Shelley.

Adie I never did.

Gary I'm so lonely.

Adie Oh, yeah.

Gary When was you like it?

Adie Last year.

Gary When you was in hospital?

Adie It was when I realised it was hopeless. That I was, that you was. The knowledge dropped like a stone. A thud. The knowledge that what I imagined could happen was false. I was falling, falling. The knowledge dropped into real knowledge. The feeling. The knowledge. Hopeless. But it can't be hopeless 'cos you're hoping. Lost all confidence. I ain't got any.

Gary You're my friend. My only one. I don't care about no one else. I don't. If only you was a girl, Adie.

Adie I don't want to be a girl, thanks.

Gary I know. But it would sort it.

Adie For you it would, mate. I've always forgiven you. You always get forgiven, you. I'll always . . .

Gary Shelley loves you.

Adie No.

Gary She do, Adie. She'll never say. But she do. Why can't you face that?

Adie I don't want to. It's Shelley. I can't.

Gary You don't like Shelley like I like you.

Adie I like her like I like her. Leave me alone.

Gary If we could divvy it all up, it would be alright.

Adie What we gonna do?

Gary Dunno.

Adie You're in charge. You are, Gary. You know that.

Gary Not of Shelley.

Adie Of me.

Gary We have to live. Live. Don't we? Best we can. Sort out what we can put up with, what we can't. Hope something comes out.

Adie Shelley won't.

Gary Shelley will have to go her own way.
Adie Don't be like that.
Gary But she will. You know that.
Adie Oh dear. Remember our field?
Gary It's nearly all gone.
Adie Our stream.
Gary Our tiddlers.
Adie And Shelley, and you, and me. Better tell your mum you're alright.
Gary Will you come with me?

SCENE NINE

The War Memorial.
    The boys bring on the statue.

Adie (*to the audience*) But we still sees Shelley. We still meets by the statue. Everyone do.
    (*to the statue*) There he is. Hello mate. Still there then, are you?

Karen and Donna come on.

Donna Don't worry Karen, he'll be out soon.
Karen How do I know? He ain't been sentenced yet.
Donna But they'll take all his time on remand off that.
Karen He might get two years. That's what he said. They found him guilty. What am I going to do?
Donna Sh. Sh. (*Sneezes.*) I always get a summer cold. See. Never in the winter.
Karen That's pollen, that is. That's hay fever.

Enter Cheesey.

Cheesey Hello, Karen. I hear Danny's going down.
Donna Shut up, Cheesey.
Cheesey Oh, sorry. What's the matter? You OK?

Donna Yes. I got . . .
Karen She got a summer cold.

Donna sneezes.
Enter Kenny and Wally.

Cheesey Hey, Wally. Where you been? I been over your house.
Wally I called for Kenny.

Enter Shelley.

Kenny Hello, Shelley.
Karen I'm not talking to her.
Cheesey She heard about Danny? You heard about Danny, Shelley?
Shelley Don't wanna hear. Mind my own business.

Enter Dumb Dumb.

Hello, Dumb.

He nods.

It's alright. It's alright.

Enter Gary and Adie.

Gary Hello, Shelley.
Shelley Hello.
Gary You OK?
Shelley Yeah.
Cheesey Where we going?
Shelley Hello, Adie.
Adie Shell. (*to the audience*) We still see each other. It's not like it was before. Gary and me, like. Yeah. That is. But we still see each other. The three of us. See how it goes, eh? See how it works out. Walk away from it. Live through it. Live with it. You can't dodge it. Can you? What you dodging? (*to Shelley*) Alright Shell?
Shelley Yeah. I'm OK.

Dumb Dumb is looking up at the statue.

Cheesey Why's he always looking at that? What is it?

Kenny War memorial.

Cheesey What's that then? What is it?

Kenny Soldier, in it.

Cheesey What is it then? What's he doing? What's he saying, then? What is he? What's he for? What's that he's reading? What's he doing? What's he for? Why is he there?

Gary It's a war memorial, Cheesey.

Cheesey What for?

Gary War.

Cheesey What war?

Shelley Men start wars.

Kenny Not in our house.

Shelley Who starts wars then?

Gary Who fights 'em?

Wally I ain't started no wars. I ain't no war starter.

Gary Who fights 'em, Shelley? Girls don't fight 'em, do they?

Adie Why did his mother let him go?

Karen Don't be stupid.

Kenny No. That's right.

Shelley Men start war.

Gary Then why don't women stop 'em, then?

Wally Yeah. Hang on, Shelley. Perhaps it's women.

Shelley How?

Wally Well, we don't know what men would be like if there wasn't no women.

Donna Don't be daft. There wouldn't be no men if there was no women.

Wally That's it then, in it?

Gary I am a boy, Shelley. I am a boy.

Shelley And I am a girl, Gary.

Kenny Peace and love. Peace and love.

Shelley Look at Adie, Gary. You got him on a piece of
string.

Gary Just because you ain't got him on a piece of string,
Shelley.

Shelley I don't want him on a piece of string. Do I,
Adie? Do I?

The soldier has dropped his letter onto the ground.

Adie Look, he's dropped the letter.
Karen What? Get out.
Adie He has.
Karen I'm going. Come on, Donna.
Donna No.
Wally What's it say?
Shelley Give here.
(*She reads the letter.*) 13 Union Street. February 12,
1915. Dear son, I got your letter and I'm glad to hear
you are well.
Gary Gis here.
(*He reads.*) Dear old chap, this is just a line to see
how you are, you old devil, and to tell you by the
time you read this I shall be joining you.

They hand the letter around and read from it.

Karen Dearest Tommy.
Cheesey Dear son.
Donna My own dearest boy.
Kenny Dear Charlie.
Wally Dear Jack.
Adie Dear Reg.
Gary Dear.
Karen Dear Harry.
Shelley I enclose some socks which I have knitted for
you.
Gary I expect it is wet where you are.
Karen The baby is doing well.

Kenny Last year we thought it would be over by Christmas.
Donna Your father got a chest, but he's still working.
Karen Mother has asked me to write to you.
Shelley Next door send their love.
Cheesey I enclose some cigarettes and that.
Donna Wish you could come home.
Wally When this is all over.
Adie Till I see you, my dear.
Shelley Your loving mother.
Karen Your loving wife.
Donna Your sister, Nelly.
Wally Your brother.
Kenny Your old friend, Wilf.
Cheesey God bless.
Karen All the best.
Donna Your loving wife.
Shelley Mary.
Gary Ted.
Adie Arthur.

> *The statue creates a series of images suggesting front line action: firing, bayoneting, holding his rifle above his head, choking, being shot, etc. These are arbitrarily juxtaposed one after the other during which the following happens*
>
> *Shelley, Karen and Donna are shocked by what they see and make sounds expressing their feelings, while Adie, Gary, Kenny, Wally and Cheesey call out the following:*

Gary Take cover.
Wally Over the top.
Kenny Shoot the officer.
Cheesey Stick the hun.
Adie Gas!
Gary Gas!

Kenny He's in the mud.
Adie I'm choking.
Kenny Send me home.
Wally Kill me.
Gary It's the rain. Steady, men.
Cheesey It's a whizz-bang.
Adie It's a shell.
Wally Fire at will.
Gary Take cover.

At the end of this, the statue takes up his usual pose.

Shelley What'll we do with this? (*Indicating the letter.*)

Dumb Dumb gives it back to the statue.

Kenny Why don't he speak?
Wally Why don't you speak? Say something.
Why can't he say something?
Gary He can't.
Shelley Why can't he? Why can't he?
Adie Are you a deserter? Did you run away? Why don't
you speak?
Dumb Dumb If he could speak, I would say I ain't
nothing. I'm nothing. I ain't nowhere. Nowhere.
There's nothing to say. Nothing. I ain't got nothing in
evidence against me, though it may harm my defence.
I got the right to silence. But I must warn me.

Online Resources for Secondary Schools and Colleges

To support the use of *Connections* plays in the Drama studio and the English classroom, extensive resources are available exclusively online. The material aims not only to make the most of new technologies, but also to be accessible and easy to use

Visit *www.connectionsplays.co.uk* for activities exploring each of the plays in a wide range of categories

- Speaking and Listening
- Writing
- Reading and Response
- Practical Drama
- Plays in Production
- Themes

Carefully tailored tasks – whether for KS3, KS4 or A-Level – are accompanied by clear learning objectives; National Curriculum links; ideas for extension and development, and for differentiation; Internet links; and assessment opportunities

The material has been compiled by a team of practising English and Drama teachers, headed by Andy Kempe, author of *The GCSE Drama Coursebook* and (with Lionel Warner) *Starting with Scripts: Dramatic Literature for Key Stages 3 & 4*

STANLEY THORNES